W9-DCL-023

The Devil in Texas

WITHDRAWN

THE DEVIL IN TEXAS

Aristeo Brito

Translated from the Spanish by
David William Foster

ANCHOR BOOKS
DOUBLEDAY
NEW YORK   LONDON   TORONTO   SYDNEY   AUCKLAND

AN ANCHOR BOOK

PUBLISHED BY DOUBLEDAY

a division of Bantam Doubleday Dell Publishing Group, Inc.
666 Fifth Avenue, New York, New York 10103

ANCHOR BOOKS, DOUBLEDAY, and the portrayal of an anchor
are trademarks of Doubleday, a division of Bantam Doubleday
Dell Publishing Group, Inc.

The Devil in Texas was originally published in hardcover by Bilingual Press/
Editorial Bilingüe in 1990. The Anchor Books edition is published
by arrangement with Bilingual Press/Editorial Bilingüe.

While the towns of Presidio and Ojinaga exist in the Rio Grande Valley, the
characters and situations in this novel are fictional and none exist in real life or are
based on persons living or dead. Any resemblance to real situations or to persons
living or dead is purely coincidental.

Library of Congress Cataloging-in-Publication Data
Brito, Aristeo.
  [Diablo en Texas. English]
  The devil in Texas / Aristeo Brito; translated
from the Spanish by David William Foster.
  — 1st Anchor Books ed.
    p.   cm.
  Translation of: El diablo en Texas.
  I. Title.
PQ7079.2.B74D513   1992   91-41780
863—dc20   CIP

ISBN 0-385-42015-3
Copyright © 1990 by Bilingual Press/Editorial Bilingüe
First Spanish edition © 1976 by Aristeo Brito and Editorial Peregrinos,
Tucson, Arizona

ALL RIGHTS RESERVED
PRINTED IN THE UNITED STATES OF AMERICA

FIRST ANCHOR BOOKS EDITION: APRIL 1992
    1   3   5   7   9   10   8   6   4   2

PQ
7079.2
.B74
D513
1992

1019

To all the Brito family

Contents

The Devil in Texas

I come from a small town called Presidio, which means prison in Spanish. It rises up dry and barren there, in the farthest corner of the earth. I'd try to describe what it's really like to you, but I can't, because it appears in my imagination as an eternal vapor. I would also like to capture it in an image for an instant, like a painting, but my mind becomes filled with long shadows, shadows that whisper in my ear, telling me that Presidio is a long way from heaven. Being born there is like being born half dead. Working there means attending to one's tasks silently, unconcerned by the fear of the tourist who comes to town and leaves frightened by the empty sound of suffering souls he hears. Perhaps these voices are what keeps me from portraying my village as it really is, for when they speak to me they shatter my head and soul as if a mad dog had played with me, leaving the remains of crumpled bodies, bodies perforated like a sieve through which the water irrigates the fields green with drunken sweat and laughter stifled by some damn uniforms with maps of the U.S. on their right arm, searching for those who soak themselves in the river that fertilizes the devil's eyes plants mocking the people and a Holy Child playing marbles on his knees while he waits for his father to come back from prison, an unknown scarecrow, a child waiting on a swing, thief of the wind, a child who hears the sighs in the water, in a fortress trembling with the howling of funereal dogs at midday, and the child dies at night, the old woman cries, a fetus thinks at night, night, night as long as infinity, a heavy night, monotonous like lying history the same as the prostitutes, although they have good reason and history doesn't, because in the pens on this side Ojinaga's skinny cows fetch a good price, to be fattened at the expense of others, and the church meanwhile is falling apart every day except on Sunday, as well as the houses of cheese and chocolate gnawed by rats because there is no cement and the ancient privies, thrones of the Catholic kings now made of tin siding and the bathrooms in the open air in the middle of winter wrapped in canvas so the eyes can't penetrate or in a bathtub in the middle of the room on Saturday to sprinkle the dirt floor, dirt-land with mounds of firewood forbidden to all except the renter who knows the bounty of the Lord who has stores that give credit for food and rationed gasoline, but medicines are not sold in the pharmacies because there are no doctors, only leaves of laurel, rosemary, rue, and mint for the children with upturned rheumy eyes, and the mothers feel as if they were in labor when they eat chorupes, beans with wild quelite, and deviled meat with azadero but penicillin cures all ills amen when the trucks loaded

with the humiliated spit at the blasphemous sun with the stench of ap-
proaching death, a smell that penetrates, penetrates, penetrates the
melted, hunched-over, broken-down spine, almost almost embracing the
melon that if you eat it it'll give you cramps if your body doesn't go
limp on you it slips away and your mind flies away in the sultry air but
be careful because they pack you off in the refrigerated Santa Fe car
and they carry you off to Disneyland while the government map asks
you if you're legal from the land sown with brothers of your brothers of
your brothers amen and the border bridge closes at midnight so a lock
can be put on hell even though the whole river used to being an owl
slips through and you don't even need the sun any longer because
you're a plant, you're barren, worn-down land, and the devil is tired of
laughing in his waterbed because the good father went at midday up the
mountain in a procession to banish him so they say and so the doors
would open along the whole river and people could cross without fear
and the cross on the top is blessed at the same time the devil is getting
ready to go out dancing and the crazy dudes can hardly sit still in the
drugstores with jukeboxes playing Elvis Presley Fats Domino Little Ri-
chard and the blob that creeps and you ain't nothing but a hound dog
finding your thrill on Blueberry Hill dancing alone with pointy shoes
with taps tapping tap tapping shoes down the street unpaved no sound
lowriders dragging their two pipes with fender skirts, skirts to cover their
shame God save us, save us, the chickens say in the chicken coops of
the houses when the cantinas close and the pool table with its broken
pockets but still ten cents a game after Tarzan movie over Tarzans wild
all over, shouts, blows on the chest on the chest of Tarzan the monkey
man who came to save the poor Indians in a school where they were
taught to fragment languages by a goatherd who taught sciences because
he knew how to drive them into dried-up pastures because the pumps
stole all the water traca traca trac the whole night long until they sucked
air and died because the cotton gin never stopped, with its whooooooo it
sucked up the trailers called the Chancla and Mocha and Golondrina
names given by the people like a stamp of possession fifty-fifty while all
the tenant farmers proud of being bosses of the lands that used to belong
to them "I pay with tools, poison, money, you kick in your life and you
give me half, that okay?" because you go and you go as hard as you
can as hard as you can and you don't earn a thing the whole year but
"how about bringing in the crop of your life? you'd never seen a thousand dollars all in one place they lie safe in a piggy bank while you

don't pay bills that add up to fifteen hundred dollars and you buy a truck without gasoline to carry your workers because you're the boss, proprietor, symbolic sower and you help the less fortunate work like dogs when you pay them part of the crumb that belongs to you from the crumb your boss paid you you humble slave, never knowing when you stepped on someone else's head it meant other peoples' heads would get stepped on in turn, God forgive them, because over on the other side, a dog's life, "hell my friend, where from?" "from Michoacán" dressed in clothes made from bags of flour and sandals with rubber soles that say Goodyear which Presidio never knew, to you, Presidio the fortunate, and to you, father who art from Presidio, Amen.

Presidio 1883

THE SNAKE, STRETCHED OUT like a tiger's tail between the candles that had gone out a long time before, begins to wiggle. The playful critter's smiling because it's the master of the world, master of this abandoned chapel, master of the rivers, of the towns situated across from each other, master of the people. And that makes it feel good.

Now it slithers along over the scapularies and the relics, numerous limbs and heads and all shapes of metallic human bodies and slips down onto the floor. With its tongue darting out it snakes slowly outside through the battered door and begins to climb toward the roof of the chapel, strangling the base of the Holy Cross. It rests for an instant in this position and then wraps itself around the top part of the cross. Now comfortably entwined, it gazes out over its surroundings. Nothing has changed, it thinks, since the friars made their way down the river many years ago. It remembers that from the very beginning they tried to cheat it, wrest its domain away, the valley that they gave the name of La Junta de los Ríos, the meeting of the rivers. But only time is permanent, it thinks. What is left of that church and that mission? Nothing.

From up there it imagines the Presidio-Ojinaga valley to be like a green arrowhead outlined by the rivers, and it is pleased with its imagination. Then it focuses on Lynch's fields, where heads pop out from time to time, and it smiles with pleasure. This time the heads are like roosters sunk among the waters of a scummy lake. The image suddenly fades with the whistle of the train crossing the bridge, and the serpent observes how, just when it's about to cross over to the Mexican side, it comes to a brief stop. Then it continues in slow motion, and the serpent smiles again. What an imagination! The river and the train: a crooked and drunken cross, a serpent cross, a melting cross. But it quickly tires of the game of images and begins to think about what it heard yesterday. That tomorrow more people are coming from the interior to work in the fields of Presidio. Stupendous! And like a child with a new toy, the serpent rapidly slides off contented. Then it begins the descent to the base of the mountain where its cave is located.

CHAVA THE IDIOT FAILED to hear the four soldiers singing. But their shouting at the mules made him jump and come out from behind a mesquite tree. Then, as if he'd seen a ghost, he threw away the skin from the banana he was eating and ran off with his hands over his ears. He didn't stop running until he reached the corner where the widow Nieves lived. Meanwhile, the soldiers were laughing uproariously over the scare they'd given the idiot until he had disappeared. After their attack of laughter died out, the mule driver ordered one of them to go announce their arrival.

"Tell Ben we got the merchandise and that we'll meet him over there at the fortín."

Sam answered by touching a hand to his cap and spurred his horse off toward the nearby house of the landowner on the outskirts of town. Meanwhile the covered wagon continued toward the fort.

Chava knelt for a long time behind the Nieves house with his eyes covered. Between Hail Marys and fits of trembling, he sang a song about a pretty little fish that refused to leave the water because its mother had told him that if he left the water, he would die right away.

When the woman heard him, she came out of her house and told him he could take his hands away from his eyes. The idiot answered her that the dead men on the mules made him hurt and that he wanted his mother.

"Stop all that right now. Would you like something to eat?"

". . ."

"Well, if you want to eat, come on in and stop biting the fingernails you don't even have."

The woman went back in, and Chava continued to pick at his face. He tried to pull out the few hairs on his chin where the skin was about to start bleeding, and he spent a few moments in serious concentration working at it. But then he began to talk to the dead, his mother Pancha, Aunt Cuca, and his fiancée Rosario. Then he decided to proceed down the street, barefoot and half naked under the 120-degree heat. "Pretty little fishy, don't you want to come and play with my hoop? We'll go out into the yard. My mother told me not to go out." But little by little Chava's song faded away along the road.

"DON'T KID YOURSELF, NEIGHBOR. Don Ben did real well this year with his harvest. That's why he's going to throw a party. Otherwise he wouldn't . . ."

"Come on, neighbor. Do you mean to say that the man has no heart?"

"No, all I mean is that it's to his advantage, since now he can afford it, and our old folks deserve it."

"You're right. They really break their backs."

"Ramón says that this time he is going to shine at the party that . . ."

"Right. He told Chindo to kill three large calves so there would be enough. There'll be two dinners. . . ."

"Really? And where's the bash going to be held afterward, neighbor?"

"Special people are coming over from Marfa. They say he even ordered five barrels of beer, the one with the star."

"But, listen, weren't they going to hold the dance there in the fort, too?"

"It doesn't look like it. . . . According to Jorge, the guy with the big snout, they're going to play in the park."

"I'm sure not going to miss it. I'm all excited, and even though my old man isn't here, I still plan on showing up. What about you?"

"Come on, do you think I'm a stick-in-the-mud? If you go, I'll go with you."

"Let's go, then."

As soon as Ben received the message, he immediately began to saddle the horse.

"No, Ben, please don't do it, for the love of God."

"And for the love of a dead dog," the old man answered as he mounted his horse.

The woman didn't answer, left alone with the sound of the hooves ringing in her ears. When the man disappeared around the bend in the road, she locked herself in, cursing her husband's anger. Rosario felt like going out into the road and shouting at the people to hang him. But she still hoped that Ben's heart would soften, and that made her calm down. She busied herself by ordering the servants to clean the tables and the party tablecloths. Ah! and that damn curtain that he'd had her make. Only Rosario knew what its purpose was, for behind it the evil of man would be hidden. She shouldn't ever forget it, he told her, but she was unwilling to take it from the cabinet, as though this action would stop the anger of her old man. Perhaps he wouldn't come for it, perhaps . . .

"PERHAPS WE SHOULD try to . . ."

"No. You do as I say."

"Sir, our orders . . . It would be better if . . ."

"No."

"Captain Ramsey said some innocent . . ."

"You tell the Captain I'm going ahead as planned. He'll get the damn thing back tomorrow. Now just help me get it into that room."

The soldiers unloaded the small cannon and rolled it toward the center of the room where Ben wanted it. Then he asked them to aim it toward the door leading to the dining room. Those who had betrayed him deserved no better than this, because they were thieves. Those bastards would see how they were going to pay for betraying him, the horse thieves.

THE NAME OF THE HORSE THIEF was Jacinto, and he had never thought about the possibility that someone had squealed on him. Thus when Lorenzo, Ben's foreman, crossed the river to bring him the invitation, he didn't hesitate at all in accepting it.

"But why so . . ."

"You deserve special treatment, Mr. Jacinto. Mr. Ben sent me expressly because he considers himself very grateful. No one has helped us so much like you and your companions. You don't forget something like that. So call them together; the party's waiting for you there. Your dinner is a special one, at eight o'clock."

Lorenzo was right, Jacinto thought, although the old tightwad would still be as miserly as ever. Otherwise, why would they be robbing him? Only in that way, by robbing him, were they able to pay themselves for the trouble they went to without receiving a just wage. But maybe Ben finally recognized the workers' worth and as a consequence invited all his friends. And by the time he'd added them up, there were twenty-five.

THAT AFTERNOON EVERYONE had a great time at the fort. But it seemed strange to them that only the salon used for serving was open. Nor could they understand why other guests like Jacinto and his men had been invited to eat later. Meanwhile, Don Benito Lynch, all decked out and smiling like an angel, chatted among the people. And thus, little by little, they forgot about the locked doors. Besides, the food was as good as the beer, and, caramba, the dancing that followed!

When the sun went down, the people scurried out into the yard where the Frontiersmen where getting ready to play, and by eight o'clock the fort was vacant. Only the special guests were left waiting for their reception. Meanwhile Chava, who had not wanted to eat, continued to crouch behind a nearby dwarf oak as though he had taken root there. He was still trembling, pensively. He remained there until the loud shot of the cannon made him run out hysterically. On the other hand, the people at the dance didn't even hear the muffled pistol shots that finished off those who were left still living. The only thing that ran through the dance that night was the rumor that a handsome stranger wearing goat's feet had been dancing.

"IN THOSE DAYS people sowed wheat, corn, things like that to be harvested before September because then the river would come and they would have to abandon their shacks out in the fields and come to the fort. The fort would be completely filled by poor people who had lost their shacks.

"Once when I was still a little girl, we planted there in the field where the best harvest was taken. We had a chile field that gave regularly because we really worked it. There was always someone to buy the chile cheap, but it was enough for us to get by. Lorenzo had a very destructive cow. He put it in a pen, and it would crawl out itself. It would get out, do its damage, and the next morning it would be back in the pen. When it would get into the irrigated chile, it would trample the shoots, and the cow stayed fat by doing us in. So Papa complained many times to Lorenzo, but Lorenzo would never admit that the cow did any damage, always asking, 'But where's your proof?' The proof, of course, was the tracks: Papa would follow the tracks back to the pen, but Lorenzo wouldn't admit to it. My papa always told him very clearly, 'Look, you'd better watch out, because I'm going to catch her, and you'll have to pay me for all the damage—go on, just take a look at what she's ruined. Just look at how the ears of corn are bent.' But no, Lorenzo's always been a real devil. Anyway, my papa went to speak to Fermín, who was the judge in those days. Fermín went to advise Lorenzo, but he got the same 'Where's your proof?' Dad told Fermín, 'We have a dog that can catch her. I'll turn the dog loose on her, and, I promise you, when he catches her the cow won't come back.' Fermín said that was fine, because he'd already told Lorenzo to control the cow or he would have to pay for the damages the animal had done, and he hadn't gotten anywhere, either.

"Well, we heard the cow. The dog obeyed my brother's orders very well, so my father spoke to him and told him the cow was out. He said, 'Turn the dog loose on her,' and he'd no sooner said it than he turned the dog loose on the cow. What a barbarian! He tore her snout to pieces and made her jump the fence. But he didn't let go, because once he'd sunk his teeth into an animal, he wouldn't let go.

"The next day, Lorenzo showed up at the house with a 30-30, cussing my papa out. My papa said, 'Hold on a minute, I'll be right there.' Then my papa went and grabbed a two-barreled shotgun. He said, 'Come on, let's see who goes first.' Well, Lorenzo backed down. And that's how the thing went."

"NOBODY LEAVES THIS WORLD, Daughter, without paying for his crimes."

"Why is Uncle Lorenzo that way, Mama?"

"Because he's full of the devil."

"But he only brought the message, Doña Mónica."

"That's not the only thing he's done, Eduvijes. You just be sure, Lorenzo is going to pay dearly for this."

"DON'T YOU THINK, Daughter, that we were that hard up. This land that Ben owns belonged to my mother Mónica, my aunt Paz, and to Victoria and Zenobio. They owned the land from here almost down to the river. In those days, my aunt Paz was mentally ill. Apolonio Varela, married to Aunt Victoria, lived in Marfa, and they came to take her to work for a while. My aunt had a small suitcase where she kept her papers to the land, and they never realized they had taken the papers away with them. She resisted being there for two or three days, but they made her sign the papers, selling to old man Ben. It was all because of her son Lorenzo.

"At that time your uncle Zenobio and the others hired a lawyer, Francisco Uranga, who we all called Don Pancho. But they told him they couldn't pay him because things were bad. But no, he told them they could pay him later. And then Ben's lawyer came in on the other side, but Don Pancho won. He said he could sell Aunt Paz's part and do whatever he wanted to, but nothing more. So Ben and Lorenzo, my aunt's son, came to an agreement. Ben greased the man's palm, gave him money, and put him to work in the riverbed. And when Papa went to work in the fields in the morning, Lorenzo had already knocked the wire fence down. Then they asked him why, and he said that it was because he was going to make it straight. That if we had beat them that time, we weren't going to again. So Uncle Zenobio, Papa, and the rest believed that since he was going to put up a berm so the river couldn't get in, it was to their advantage. Lorenzo was the slick one, and he screwed things up. He was so heartless that he cheated the crazy old woman, his own mother. May God forgive him, Daughter."

No ONE EVEN KNEW how they got to Presidio, but the fact is that they were riding horses and shouting. They came from the south of Texas with one idea: to bury the people alive and to thrust them even deeper into hell. And even though the invaders had come to the darkest corners of the earth, they knew how to be creative. In Presidio they discovered that the land and the people had lucrative possibilities, but some of them had to be buried first. A few months later, they went straight down to the river to drown the launch operator, Don Pancho's son, in the water. First because he had struck Ben, and second because there were larger interests in the transportation of people. But the only thought on Jesús's mind was his sister Rosario. What business did that bastard gringo have dating her? Come on! Stay the hell away! So one night they buried Jesús under water, filling the launch and his body with dirt so the two would stay submerged. The stone hung from his neck would make sure of that. Meanwhile, his lawyer's diploma was only good for Don Francisco to wipe his ass with, since the case was thrown out of court. And the worst part was that his daughter ran off with the gringo before the year was out. Shit! Not only down, but out as well! But from now on, watch out, you bunch of bastards! Later, his brother Santamaría continued to ferry people across even after they said there would soon be an international bridge, and as soon as it was built, people would have to use it to get across. But Santamaría, armed with a carbine, ignored that law because people preferred the launch. Go through the checkpoint and show papers? Go straight to hell. The bridge was the work of the devil. (The bridge is the devil's rainbow: two goat's feet with each one planted in a graveyard. The bridge is a slide to make you die laughing, right, Jesús?)

"THE LYNCHES HAVE THEIR HISTORY; the old people, anyway. They killed people like barbarians. There were some poor people working for them, and when they tried to leave after a year, they took their pay with them. Sure, I'll pay you, they would tell them, but then they would take them away and kill them. People didn't protest because there was nothing to eat. Things were very bad. Around here we had to get by on cups of atole or whatever. So what could anyone do about it? Sure, there were men like Papa who weren't bothered by having to kill someone. And so there were men like him who could do whatever they wanted to with anyone they wanted to, but they would think about not leaving the families all alone. Because anyone can be courageous. But Papa was all tied down with us. Otherwise, how long would the Lynches last? You could just chop their heads off and cross over to the other side. Because don't think there were only Lynches around here. I can still remember how that Captain Gray used to kick ass. He belonged at that time to the Texas Rangers. He was real mean."

DON PANCHO COULDN'T UNDERSTAND the broken message that Chava the idiot was giving him, so he did his best to calm him down. Once he had calmed down a little, he opened the store's storage room and spread a sarape over the bags of beans so Chava could lie down. At least he won't spend the rest of the night wandering around in a daze, Francisco thought. Then he put the chain on the door and went home to his house-store-printshop, certain that truth would come out with the light of day.

But the night turned out to be a long one for Pancho. A few hours later a pair of eyes full of pure rage showed up at his door. Reyes handled the carbine as though it were made of paper; at the same time he poured out of the corner of his mouth the story of what happened at the fort. When he finished, the old man invited him in, but Reyes refused. He said he preferred to go find out the truth, since Chindo's word was often unreliable.

"Okay, but don't go doing anything foolish."

"That creep'll get his."

"Make sure first, Son, and be patient."

"That's what I'm going to do, make real sure."

"Then we'll talk about it. But don't forget, Reyes. It's never too late as long as you're still alive."

"Okay, old man."

Don Pancho went into his private office and there among books and piles of newspapers, he set about struggling against his cynicism. He meditated on his life and his career, which had been a real disaster. Nothing more. Failure, crashing failure, period. The dusty newspapers and books that surrounded him were the last vestiges of a fight he'd lost. Proof of his creative age? Even the question was stupid. He remembered how his own destruction matched the town's, how the two had been reduced to an insignificant microcosm, but one replete with history. For his part, he had been spurned by both governments because of his strong sense of justice. There was nothing left of the efforts he had made during his time to ensure basic human rights, and the only thing that consoled him was unearthing his truth buried under the dust. The issues of *The Frontiersman* he had saved in his office said it all. Perhaps someone would come someday and read them, but that would be after he was dead.

He remembered very well his first year of practice, because it was in that same year when the world he had built in the air during his studies collapsed around him. Reality, damn it, was something else. Life was lived by shouting and waving hats. He had soon realized that the career of a lawyer was not quite so illustrious, and even less when it was practiced in a town of impoverished conditions. Then he came to realize that the best way to help others and to help himself would be through journalism, and he immediately began to publish *The Frontiersman*, a small newspaper that was read not only by those who needed to read it but also by other publishers in the Southwest. His undertaking grew strong when to his surprise he began to receive newspapers from California, Trinidad, Colorado, Laredo, New Mexico, and from places where he never even suspected there were Mexicans. In time, the publication became a strong voice with one concern: polemics, denunciation, and protest over the life of Mexicans in these areas. Soon his words were being picked up by newspapers in Mexico, and the Mexican government did not take long to recognize Francisco Uranga's benefit to the country. He received his appointment as consul with great enthusiasm. The exact words? "To serve as representative of our citizens abroad as appropriate in the defense of their rights and principles as designated by the treaties between Mexico and the United States." Just as soon as he had received the appointment, he began to order by priority the tasks to be undertaken. First, the clarification of the question of properties that had been usurped in the Presidio valley and to discover how to validate claims on lands that had little by little been rolled away like a rug. (But he remembered that by that time it was already too late because the legal archives were written in another language and bore another seal.) Later, he would pursue the complicated question of citizenship, and for that he would have to contact the other consuls in the Southwest. And he would have to find quickly a more efficient way of arranging the repatriation of all those individuals who wished to go home, but who thought that the Mexican government had abandoned them. Another of the causes, and here he was emphatic, was the need to combat the insolence on the part of those who considered themselves the law, and crossed the border without prior authorization. This point was one of the touchiest, because he had seen numerous cases in which the person being pursued was taken out of Mexico in order to try him in a foreign court and in a foreign language. Yes, it was necessary to clarify the law of extradition so trammeled by the conqueror, although he knew that it was a very difficult task. On other occasions, the opposite occurred: the person accused by the Mexican authorities could not prove that he was a citizen of the United States, even when the treaty said that anyone not repatriated within two years would be considered a citizen. And the papers? They had vanished into thin air. Where are you from? From the land, sir. From wherever I can make a living.

It did not take long for Pancho Uranga to realize that he was in the same whirlpool. Between the accumulation of paper and the confusion, he lived as though sick and lost at sea. He ended up with his hands tied with frustration, transformed into one of those persons who know so much about how the world works that they smirk as if to say: Jerks, what did you expect? God's blessings wrapped in a blanket? Get it straight; humanity is rotten to the core. And each time the devil won out, the thorn dug deeper, and by the time he tried to extract it, it had already poisoned his soul. By then he had taken up the pen as a sword. His writings appeared in his own paper, *The Frontiersman*, in *The Tucsonian*, *The Spanish American*, *The Zurtian*, *The Voice of the People*, and forty other newspapers that were coming out at that time: "I roundly denounce the usurpation of the lands and I support the White Caps for having shown their weapons"; "I put my name to the resolution of the unified Spanish American press which condemns the governor of New Mexico for calling us 'greasers' in the English-language press of New York and who now has the nerve to threaten us"; "I protest the filibustering expeditions of opportunistic Yankees"; "I condemn discrimination in the workplace, in schools, and in public establishments"; "I support the defenses mounted by the Mexican Alliance"; "with anger and love I lament the dissolution of our people and I weep for its future"; "I am a partisan of the radical element of workers in San Antonio, California, and New Mexico, not because I know they have achieved something, but because it proves that we are still alive and that there will be something for us to fight"; "I am suspicious of the justice and the sentences meted out by judges that are guided by the opinions of prejudiced witnesses; moreover, I know that Manuel Verdugo was not guilty. I found out afterward that he was sentenced to die in El Paso"; "I condemn the sale of black slaves in Fayetteville, Missouri"; "for the information of the editor of the aforementioned rag in Guadalajara, my efforts to repatriate our people are genuine. And I do so because I know the sufferings experienced in a country that is considered the best example of democracy, and I also would have you understand fully, via examples, that our people here are not a bunch of tamale vendors, as you so grossly describe us. The survey I print here contains the number of persons of Mexican descent, and you should know that of all those who responded, only four are in the business of selling tamales, and not because they are lazy but because of the adverse fortunes they have experienced. I have on numerous occasions appealed to the Mexican government to provide the money to provide transport for those who want to be repatriated, as well as to allot them a parcel of land; otherwise, what guarantee is there that they would live any better if they returned to Mexico? The problem now has its roots in the fact that the Chinese are willing to work for less wages"; "I would have the gentleman, who speaks without any basis when he says that those of us who are from here are the poorest and uneducated, know that, if we concede that he is right that the working family lives poorly, that doesn't mean we are uneducated. We recognize our circumstances and do what we can about them. Now, explain to me, Mr. Publisher, why you believe that these working people are the ones who least seek to be repatriated? On another occasion I would like you, instead of spewing out nonsense, to set yourself to thinking a little more. We, my colleague, do not wish to move from this land that we have always considered our own, and if I make the effort to repatriate some people, it is because I am moved by the hope that the Mexican government will help us"; "I would remind the governor of Chihuahua that he made a big mistake by conceding vast areas of land to the settlement companies, since all they do is take over the natural resources. In time these companies will go the same way as the great overlords who now exploit the poor mercilessly"; "I denounce publicly the misguided deeds of the consul in El Paso, who cooperated with the sheriff in the extradition of Rufino Gómez. The hundred pesos they paid him under the table will not serve to calm his conscience after the accused has been sentenced"; "I would never have believed that one of our own (from Laredo) would comment so unfavorably on the poetry that we publish in the literary section, and even less so over its being written in 'bastard' Spanish. We regret very much that these attitudes are so deeply rooted. Why is our colleague so blind to the facts? Better, why doesn't the gentleman lodge his complaints with the educational system or the federal government, which promised to respect our language and our culture? If there were schools where our maternal tongue were taught, perhaps you would have no reason to complain. But this is an ideal. You'd be better off to spend your energies in assuring the well-being of your children, since God knows they need it, rather than showing the same attitude of superiority that we have experienced for so long."

Thus he pricked sensitivites with the tip of his pen, and it wasn't too long before both governments considered him an enemy of harmony. By the time he defended the cause of Catarino Garza, who provoked the uprising of workers in New Mexico against the landowners and the government of Chihuahua, he had ceased to be consul. It was a miracle he wasn't killed, although in those days he would have preferred it, because nothing mattered to him. The town he had defended with love now turned its back on him, and that was what hurt the most. Some, as soon as luck went their way, came down on him. "Old troublemaker, leave well enough alone. Things are going well, and you threaten our position with your stupidity. So either you shut up or . . ." *The Frontiersman* died a death without glory. People were right, history stops for no one. (History flows like water. Sometimes calm, sometimes with the devil riding it, making it swollen and rabid. Then it brings forth a deformed hand that stretches its fingers out to infinity. Then the water's hand withdraws and becomes a claw, leaving only a trickle in the bed of the Río Grande. Then the people on their eternal migration return to form a twisted cross, a miserable cross of flesh and water.) And since the history of my race is that of the river, I thought, I am going to build a launch to ferry them across. This will help me support myself, but I will charge only those who can pay. It will also give me the opportunity to guide people by setting them on the best road. "Go this way and be careful with this and that, and if he doesn't give you a job, follow the river until . . ." But before I do that, I'll gather my belongings, my books, and move to Ojinaga. I will build a house near the river on the other side, in order for our history not to be washed away in the water. Many years after, when I lost Rosario and I found out they were going to build the bridge, I wasn't even surprised. Not even when I heard that they had drowned my Jesús. My wound began to bleed again when he was buried a mess, and I swore I would avenge him. But I couldn't, and I thought you would avenge him, Reyes, being his brother. I didn't want really to raise you to be an assassin. The weapons would come later, and these only as a last resort. What I wanted to give you first was book-learning, but not out of those that tell false stories. That's why I had you study with Mariana, my teacher, and not in that hovel of a school where they drill you with the idea that you should cut off the roots of the language that gave you birth. Then I would send you there to Presidio, but only after you knew the truth, why things are the way they are, when you would be proud to be a son of the people. But as you well know, you turned out a failure. I don't know why you were that way since childhood, Reyes. When I sent you to Mariana, after only a few days she came to tell me you had hit her back after she had struck you. I never even wanted to see your face. You didn't want to go to school, even though it earned you a lot of whippings; do you remember, Reyes? I still don't know how you learned what you do know. Perhaps from my books that you read on the sly, because I never saw you bother with anything. You're lazy and a bum. Busy yourself with the firewood so you can buy and sell or go help your uncle Santamaría with the launch, I told you, but no, you'd show up in the afternoon with food, firewood, and money. "And where did you get that money?" "I sold fish to the gringo down the bridge." "I told you not to go messing around with them! Damn kid!"

THE GALLOPING OF THE FIVE horses was cushioned by the loose sand of the river. The horsemen drew up to the shore, plunging themselves into the mud until they could reach the water. The boy Reyes was playing absentmindedly, and he didn't hear a thing because of his splashing in the water. The men looked at each other and smiled, ready to give him a good scare, but at that moment a horse couldn't fight off a tickle in his nose and snorted. The boy jumped like a fish struggling against the hook, and the men burst out laughing.

"Just look at the little devil. Come over here. Where are you from?"

"From here, from that house over there."

"Who's your father, and what does he do?"

"Francisco Uranga, Don Pancho, the man who runs the launch."

"Do you know this place well? Do you know where the gringos live?"

"Yes. This is where they killed my brother."

"Why did they kill him?"

"I'm not sure, but they say because it's against the law not to use the bridge."

"Fucking bastards. They still believe this land belongs to them. Just because it's on the other side of this damn puddle. And what the hell are you doing hanging around here?"

"I was fishing."

"All you're going to catch is a cold, dumb kid. Do you want to go with us? What do you say, boys? Can we use him?"

"Sure, why not, Chief?"

"Come on then, get dressed, and congratulations."

"No, sir, I don't want to go with you, and my father wouldn't . . ."

"Cut that stuff out. What the hell good is there in hanging around here?"

"Ramón, hand me that good one. There you are. Now then. Listen, I just know this is going to turn out right."

"The kid looks like an owl with such a large carbine and his eyes popping out, Chief."

They all laughed. Reyes didn't know that at that moment his brother Jesús was coming alive in him and that the indignation of half a century would begin to take shape that very day.

"I DIDN'T WORK IN SHAFTER, but when I was a girl, my sister Camila married Cipriano Alvarado and said, 'Don't stay here, let's go.' Then she sent for me and my brother Chente, but I told her real clear, 'I'm not going to spend all my time with you.' She said, 'Fine. Whenever you want to come, I'll go for you.' There were a lot of people in Shafter in those days, along with a lot of money because the silver mines were working. The men earned so much that even my little brother got the fever, as little as he was. But that's how it was with the poor. They died. When they went down into the mines, they came out sick, the poor devils. I think that's what my brother Chente died of."

"WHY DO I HAVE TO DIE, Eduvijes? Sister, I'm only twelve years old. That's no reason to cry. You've done what you could. I only want to know what life is like when you grow up. But you're grown up. Tell me, is life pretty, like it is when you're a child? That's how it seems to me, Vicke. . . . Vicke, your name, Eduvijes, is pretty, too, but I like Vicke better. . . . Last year when my dog died, I felt very bad, if only you could've seen me, because his eyes were very sad and he was still wagging his tail. Did you know that dogs wag their tails when they're happy? Is it true that he was happy, Vicke? When he was dying? Even when I'd hit him, he'd wag his tail. Are grown-ups like you? I felt very bad before he died, because I had hit him too. And before he died, I promised him I wouldn't do it again. Because I believe that no one has the right to hit you, to strike you, and if they do, you ought to hit them back. Because then you die and go to heaven without getting even. Well, that's what I used to think, Vicke, but not now. Because I believe that if the dog is so full of love like that, people must have even more. I say that because I feel more love than the dog, Vicke. Is that how it is with you? Damn it! You're crying! Don't cry, Vicke. Give me a smoke. I've never smoked, but now I want to see what it's like to smoke. Come on, light it for me. I wish you could wipe this sickness away, Vicke, the lump I have here in my chest. It sure hurts. Look, touch me here. I wish you could remove it. I want to cry, Vicke, but what would Don Jesús say? It would make me feel ashamed. What did he use to say? That men don't cry. Is that true, Sister? I wouldn't tell you this if he were here, but look, once I found him crying behind a tree. I never knew why, but if he saw you crying, he would carry you in his launch. Do you remember, before the bridge was built, how he would take people from one side to the other? I used to have a lot of fun with him. In those days we were all equal. It's not that we aren't anymore, but things have changed since they built the bridge. It's funny, Vicke. People feel apart. Aren't bridges supposed to be for just the opposite? Before, we could go see Grandma and Grandpa without . . . What are those papers for, Vicke? Why do those men ask for them all the time? Who are they? Have you ever seen the devil, Vicke? Is it true we're in hell? It's sure hot here, but this isn't hell, right, Vicke? My grandma told me that the devil lived in that cave where we went, do you remember? I don't believe it, because it's been blessed up there on the sierra. But they told me that he came to do us evil, that he was all over the river. Vicke, you're not talking. My chest hurts a

Bridge

lot. Bring me a warm rag, please. This cigarette is no good. I thought it would take the pain away. Why am I sick, Vicke? Why don't they make me feel better, please? When you come back, Vicke, get me into bed. I'm not comfortable here on the floor. I don't know why they put me down here. Vicke, I don't want to die!"

Night stretches out toward infinity. Like a black and sticky piece of gum that envelops the river, the trees, the fields. Then it reaches down to the houses and wraps itself around the people, gluing them firmly to their beds, the floor, or wherever they were caught sleeping. The silence is also dark and monotonous. Then the moon comes out, emerging with the rhythm of the violins, and the gum turns into mercury, laying a slippery coating down over the universe. The river is platinum-colored, the leaves of the poplars are silver, and everything is silver-colored like a snowy night in other climes.

Silver gives dimension to the night. It lengthens and multiplies the night. The moon is not death. The moon is life for the people swarming around the river. The shadows take on life under the moon. There is the moon, eating a cactus fruit, casting the peels to . . . Moon, give me some, give me what you are eating. You are my life and my adoration. I am you, moon. Your shadow. I am the body that lights up the night, that stretches the night out. I am a man of night, I am the life of night. I am the son of She Who Weeps, and my name is Reyes, sons of bitches. I am the brother of Jesús of the river.

In the deepest part of the cave situated in the depths of the sierra of Santa Cruz, a ray of light falls on a still pool of water. The serpent uses it as a mirror, a mirror that now reflects a human face. The image contemplates the mask full of laughter; a dark blue suit, a cap to cover his pointy head where horns are usually seen, and some shiny boots, also black. The boots don't fit right on his rooster feet, but that's not important. It's only for a few hours. As a final touch, the "stationmaster" serpent takes down an oil lamp set aside for this occasion. Now he's all ready to show up at the train station. Later, he'll exchange his mask for that of a ranch hand, but only when he's ready to receive the five hundred souls of the workers coming in from the interior. Once outside, the devil in human form mounts his burro and heads him toward the station.

The train station for beyond the grave is almost empty when he gets there. That's strange, since there are always swarms of people waiting for trains. Perhaps they've finally realized they never run on time. The ticket seller confirms this to him. "The train's running a few minutes late," he says. That's what he says, but the devil knows very well that the word "minute" doesn't mean a thing. That's why there are warnings fastened to the wall: *Trains running to paradise leave on the hour, but their arrival depends on the will of God.* The other warning corresponding to the line to hell is also emphatic: *These trains run according to the will of man and arrive when least expected.* Dumb, stupid people. It looks like they never read what's obvious.

It's the first time the devil in human form has been in a train station, and he feels the same expectation that a passenger or a spectator experiences. He has also heard that the trains run late, and since he's not used to waiting, he begins to have doubts about himself. Now he's not so sure he heard the announcement right, that today and at this hour the workers would arrive. "No, it's not possible for me to be wrong. I'm real sure that the travelers departed. There's never any doubt about that. But perhaps? . . . The devil-man goes over to read the announcements to see if by chance the information they contain will ease his doubts. "Let's see. . . ." He reads, but it doesn't really help. Just stupidities: ". . . return tickets are not sold on the line to paradise; children under seven travel free in their mothers' arms; there are no reduced fares; only good works can be carried as baggage in order to avoid being detained; travelers of any nationality are allowed as long as their passports are in order; the central ticket office is open around the clock." Fools! Nothing more! The line to paradise went out of business a long time ago. The devil then moves on to the announcement concerning hell: "No discounts, no minors, passengers may travel with as much luggage as they want, but they must leave everything but their soul behind. . . ." Ah! Here it is! ". . . *those who travel on this line may continue on the line to paradise if a priest stamps that they've confessed on their tickets before changing to the death train.*" Son of a . . .! Can it be possible?

What if the train got stopped out there, precisely for this reason? Could there be some miserable party-pooper? Could there?

"The train's pulling in on track number five."

The few people begin now to stir while the masked man stands there astonished. He hasn't even heard the puffing of the train.

"Please, ladies and gentlemen. Exercise caution. Please do not approach until the train has come to a complete stop."

The devil stationmaster, lamp in hand, follows the bunch of people so excitedly that he has forgotten to change his clothes. "Now to detour those wearing huaraches," he thinks.

The passengers begin to get off the train. One, two, three . . . then two . . . then . . . one. . . . They can be counted on one hand. The train is empty. No, it can't be. The stationmaster doesn't know what to think, and he stands there for a long time until no one else gets off.

"But where are all the other people?"

"That's all there are, sir."

"Look here. There were supposed to be . . ."

"I told you there are no more. Don't pester me!"

The stationmaster turns red with anger and makes a screeching sound as he smashes the lamp against the track. Then he lets loose with a fart that could never have smelled human, disappearing like a flash into the heavens. The burro is left braying for its master, while at the corner of the station the Los Pepenados group sings: "The devil went for a walk . . . and they gave him chocolate . . . it was so hot that he burned his craw . . . it was so hot he burned his craw . . . but ay, hah, hah, hah . . . hah hah hah hah . . . but ay, hah hah hah hah . . . hah hah hah hah hah. . . ."

THE FIVE HUNDRED ACRES of cotton were about to be lost because of a lack of pickers. It had been Ben's first blow, and the situation grew worse when the people from Presidio demanded a penny more for each pound picked. There was no way to explain who had had enough influence to cut him off. Besides, the "incident" at the fort was so insignificant in proportion to the business he conducted that he had forgotten it that very night. Previously, an act of justice like this had not kept the water from flowing calmly and lucratively. Why should it be different on this occasion?

What could have happened? Why had the government refused to allot him the five hundred souls he'd requested? He had no answer. He could not explain how the excursion that Governor Jones, his friend, had made to Mexico had failed.

Only Francisco Uranga and his son Reyes had the answer, and when the latter read the news in Marfa's *Century*, the tears flowed. They were tears of triumph that had waited for so many years, and they were tears of pleasure because his triumph had been double. The Mexican administration knew full well the mistreatment of its workers, but there were always more beneficial moves, and it was easier to hide things with money. Hell! It was just because of that that Don Pancho couldn't believe it. To have brought them to their knees was almost unbelievable!

How had it happened? When he had learned that Jones would almost certainly be the next governor of Texas, Francisco had gone to Marfa to shake his hand. There, the day he had come to play the clown in public, he had found out about his "international" intentions. He immediately availed himself of the newspaper fraternity to begin to pick away in earnest. First, he informed the publishers from around here: Rodríguez of the *Zuriago*, Sifuentes of the *Laredian*, Armenta, Armendáriz . . . from then on he'd become the voice of a network that had no boundaries. It had been easy. To make public the massacre at the fort and, right after, to outline Jones's excursionist plan.

They waited for Jones at each stop in Mexico and hammered him with the same question: "Is it true that the Mexican suffers in Texas, more than in any other state, discrimination in the workplace and in other public establishments? Is that business about the massacre in Presidio true? I'm asking this question because so-and-so corroborates that . . ." By the time the Governor reached the capital three days later, his head was spinning. Martínez-Vega, the consul in Matamoros, had shown up at the official convention and requested the floor. First he gave the details and background of how he had confronted the governor himself, and then he went right on to read a list of accusations. Finally, he read a resolution signed by the principal Spanish-language publishers of the Southwest. The pressure and the scandal assumed such proportions that the corrupt policeman Alcalá had to refuse publicly Jones's request to export workers to the State of Texas. It was quite a joke, Francisco thought, that only weeks before, the Mexicans in Arizona had heeded the call of the governor of that state. "We need the support of every good citizen for our crops not to be lost." The first ones to turn out had been those who spoke Spanish, forming troops of people to salvage the harvest on Sunday. One paradox after another. Christ!

BENITO LYNCH WELCOMED THE NEWS by slaughtering a kid goat that had gotten in his way. Later, like Don Quixote, he rode by on horseback, knocking over the tents that he had bought for the occasion. They couldn't even stand him at home for those five days.

Nevertheless, Benito had not allowed himself to be beaten. He ordered Lorenzo to announce to the local workers that they would get the raise they requested. Meanwhile, since he was in a bind, he would personally go over to the other side to insist that they be paid a good price for harvesting the cotton. After the man had made his offer before the various assemblies, Reyes, for his part, gathered his comrades together and ordered them to make another, contrary, announcement publicly, written in the form of a warning: "Crossing the river is forbidden for anyone who intends to work in Benito's fields. Any act that supports the cause of this criminal will be punished severely. The Coyote." No one showed up in the fields on the second day, except for Lorenzo, who brought the announcement to his boss's house.

"And who is this Coyote?"

"I don't know, boss. It's the first time I've heard the nickname. But what I find out is that there's been a band of thieves for some time and they have no qualms about going after what they want."

"So, that's the way it is, huh? Fine. You go to Mexico and announce that I will pay four cents for each pound picked and that I will provide complete armed protection."

He went on to inquire about the whereabouts of the Coyote. He didn't care who he was. All he wanted was to waste him.

Lorenzo was back that same day before too long. He brought two items of information: first, that he had succeeded in obtaining twenty nighttime pickers for him, pickers who were a little unsure about even wanting to do it. In any case, he had told them if they decided to come, one of them should come and say they're coming at night. The second item of news was that the Coyote was none other than Reyes Uranga, his brother-in-law. No kidding! Reyes, the quietest of the whole pack of hands. Reyes? That made him laugh.

Benito lost no time in going into action. He got in touch immediately with the sheriff in Marfa for him to come and help out, and by the third day he was already poking around the houses and outskirts of Presidio. Then, after they found nothing on this side, the ten rangers crossed the river to the Mexican side and went up to the sierra where they supposed that Reyes and his band were hidden. But they came away from there, too, with empty hands. Thus, the following day they announced they were leaving, preparing their departure with dimmed lights, and by night they returned to see if by chance . . . But Reyes had not swallowed the hook.

Nothing happened the fourth day either, but a wetback showed up at night at Ben's house to tell him that the twenty that had been recruited were on their way. But it would not be that night, but the following one. So Ben prepared the sacks and left them by the trunk of the fat tree near the water pump. Benito did not tell Lorenzo that the wetback had come, out of fear that the plan would be discovered. Neither the wetback nor the pickers knew they were the bait. The strategy was simple. To get Reyes where he was weak, by mistreating the people a little bit, and if he had any balls, the bastard would come out in the open. What Benito did not know was that Reyes himself had practiced with the pickers the day before. Did they want to work? Okay, then either fish or cut bait, he had told them. They would have to cooperate. So what if they got hit by a bullet? They'd get what they deserved.

BENITO SMILES as he walks among the dark houses. Not even any dogs are barking, or maybe he can't hear them. He smiles with triumph written on his lips. His smile, made from a grimace that fools no one, is as clear as an X-ray. The rider moves among the blocks of prosaic adobe. Adobes that were made at one time from new straw and that now look like useless cornstalks. Anybody who'd want to make poetry of this is a liar. All the houses lack is a cross in front of them to be cemeteries. Nevertheless, now and then one of them wards off death with little flowers and a veranda in front. Then the dusty, unblack-topped street. The green devil smiles because they've all been tricked. The devil manipulates puppets. The devil plays with human life. And human beings never understood how he made it into their midst. He was like a gust of wind that blows between their legs, making them trip. Others say that it was a dream from which they had awakened naked. When they awoke, they had placed themselves in the hands of the gentleman, who had promised them relief and had made good. He had given them work on their own land, and the people began to feel life again in their stomachs. Then he paid them in advance, and they paid it back into his hands. "Every family gets a box of food as a Christmas gift, and I'll have a barbecue when the harvest is over. But don't forget, vote for me, vote Democratic." In two years, the vassals had crowned a king they called the "Green Devil."

A stifling night, an oppressive night, a night that chokes people. Pale skulls of squeezed-out sap, skulls lost on the dry land of the cotton fields. False plants watered with sweat. Stuffed worms. Presidio, prison, hell. A devil laughing silently. Shhh!

Benito appeared like a ghost at the door of the house. Then he glued his lips to the jamb and called quietly . . . "Pst! Lorenzo!"

The barking of the dog inside the porch answered him, and Benito jumped back.

"Shut up, you bastard!"

"Hey, who's there?"

"It's me, Ben."

"Wayda momen."

"That's okay, Lorenzo. Don't get up. I'm only here about the pickers. They're near the river. Go by later, okay?"

"Okay, Don Benito."

The Green Devil moved away like a shadow.

Lorenzo did not go to bed then. The appearance of Ben at this hour had left him restless, so he went outside to smoke a cigarette. Crafty old guy, bastard. If he weren't paying my salary, I would have bailed out already. The problems he brings me. One of these days I'm going to wake up stretched out in the river, plugged by my own people. And people are right, I'm bad to them, but the fact is that they get you from all sides. If the old goat helped the poor people instead of paying them shit, he wouldn't have any problems. Jerk. Some day he'll change, after I'm good and dead.

ALREADY IN THE MIDDLE of the field ten riders appear and surround old Ben. He tells them the basics: the pickers will be in the section indicated by the fat poplar, but to be on the safe side, wait for Lorenzo. The latter didn't need a pistol to convince him he should serve as guide. Just don't go too far. Then we'll see what happens, he tells them.

The man digs his spurs in and disappears into the night. It's been a long day.

THE WHISTLE ON THE OTHER SIDE of the river shatters the silence. It reaches the ears on the Mexican side. Quickly various figures jump into the river and lose themselves among the cotton fields. Like frightened criminals they run toward the poplar tree to grab the bags and disappear again into the ditches. They tie the bags to their waists and begin to devour the plants like locusts. Bush after bush is stripped. *Shas. Shas. Shas.* The bags fill up. They cast the bag over their shoulders like a giant sausage and place it alongside the ditch.

This night the pickers are especially wary and move filled with fear. Worse, they don't know if it's the waiting or not being sure if the Coyote will come. For that reason some of them have started in the middle of the rows and have picked toward the river.

The men drag themselves along under the moonlight. They twist and turn among the plants. The green plants, with their white buds, look like Christmas trees. The pickers try to climb to the top just like elves. But they can't escape the long tail that ties them to the ground. Now the serpent, tied to their waists, tries to devour them with its open maw, but it can't. The picker stuffs it with cotton, cocoons that will leave it full so it will leave the people alone. The rapid, rapid hands get all scratched. Perhaps some miracle will transform the cocoons into small gold coins. But it's all no use. The devil carts them away. The devil multiplies. Then another serpent comes along, as hungry as the other one and then another and another, until one night God's blessing pays them for the misery they don't deserve. For now the platinum-colored pickers will continue to slither among the green sea and white serpents. White tufts, poof, greenbacks. Green eyes, green teeth. Rotten, the soul rotten, green, green. Green sea, green bodies, green death, decomposition.

FRESH DEATH in an upholstered coffin is nice and warm. The body can lie down in it, enjoy the warmth of an electric blanket. But these moments are short-lived because then the evening's dew takes its place and envelops the body in cold. That is when the soul emerges with the will to prolong life. It slips along the upholstery like a cat seeking warmth, but it's all useless; the coffin's no longer warm or tender. The soul is like a mother who loses her son in a storm, and the wind carries her far away from her lost child. That's what happens with Chente. The dawn's breeze transforms his soul into a long trail of cigarette smoke, blowing it over toward the fort, where so many other souls have been deposited.

OUTSIDE, BEHIND THE HUT, the men squatted on their haunches around a bottle. As the couples would arrive at the house of the deceased, men and women would separate and go off in different directions. The women would go in; the men would enlarge the circle. With the warmth of the bottle and Levario's animated tongue, the men often forgot why they were there.

Inside, there is a wafting odor of wax, but it is soon blanketed by the dust rising from the dirt floor. No faces can be seen in the dying light of the candle. Rather, there are bodies wrapped in black dresses and shawls like fishnets. The women who were able to find a seat stare off into space. They are like mummies, tired of fingering their rosaries. It looks like they are trying to make the beads rounder and, at times, as if someone had wound them up, they begin to pray out loud. The murmuring lasts only a few minutes; then there is a leaden silence, a silence interrupted by a huge and bothersome fly. The fly buzzes twice around the coffin of the deceased and lands. Silence takes over again. The women get up to go out for some air and others come in to take their places on the benches. Shrouded rows contrast with recently whitewashed walls. Roberto, Eduvijes's fiancé, comes and goes, comes in and goes out, asking the men to help him bring chairs from their houses because more people are likely to show up. Thanks to Chito, Levario, Don Francisco, and Reyes, who came and left

early, everyone's helped him out. Poor Vicke didn't even have
time to make her dress, sweep, make arrangements. But everyone
helped out. The coffin, placed on top of two buckets, was donated
by Levario, despite the fact that he was so repulsive. You had to
know him to stand him. He was one of those persons who only
need to open their mouths to give you a pain in the ass. The
announcement on the door of his "coffin factory" says it all:
DIE IN STYLE . . . WITH LOMELI COFFINS. But he had a good
heart. Roberto remembers the time he went to fetch a coffin for
the little angel:

"Who was it this time?"

"Chentito, Vicke's brother."

"Ah! May he rest in peace, since he never got any here. The
kid was born sick. He almost died when he was six months old,
and the worst part is that all they gave him to eat was crackers
with coffee. Let's see, how about these, they're the best ones.
He'll sure go to heaven in style with this one, right? Heh, heh.
With this upholstery he can fly pdq. Take it, no charge, and tell
Vicke many happy returns, hah, hah. That's right, tell her I'll
stop by to see her tonight." (That's the reason, you talk too much,
and because you are what you are, you rub people the wrong way,
jerk. Maybe also because you joke about death, making fun of it.
Look at you, dressed in your best, with your bottle of tequila ready
to yak all night long. That's what you'll do until your wife Virginia stops you cold and drags you drunk off home. I don't like
you because you're a parasite of death.)

"Thanks, Levario. God bless you."

THE HUT IS LITTLE, but the whitewash makes the two rooms look
bigger. The percale curtain covers the opening where the door
should be, although the light shines through as it does from the
priest's side of the confessional. Vicke, sitting on her bed, observes the movements with dull eyes and then casts her gaze on a
candle that threatens to go out as it projects the heart of Jesus
along the wall. Christ accompanies Vicke in her suffering, a suffering that flickers in tune with the dancing light. The Holy
Child, with his luxurious garment, is also present. Now Vicke
moves her gaze to the portrait of the dead little angel and then to
the image of the Holy Child. Once, twice, three times. Many

times, until the two images become one. She studies and com-
pares them. The curly hair, the smile, the joined hands. "Ay, no,
no, the picture is missing a hand!" And she recalls that it was because of the wind last night. She remembers that when the statue
fell, her brother was dying, the poor thing. She had picked the
statue up from the floor, as he had ordered her to, and no sooner
had she done it when the child became very talkative. When she
brought him the warm cloth he'd requested, he asked her to take
him by the hand, and then be began to remember things. "Let's
see, Vicke, I'll bet you don't remember this: there's the moon . . .
What's that business about the moon eating prickly pears if it's
made of cheese? I believe that if it were true, it would've already
melted, don't you think so, Vicke? There's the sun drinking so-
tol. . . . Listen, Vicke, do you think things in heaven are like us?
That's why I'm not afraid of the night, are you? When you go
outside, I don't . . . the snake in the sea, in the sea, around here
you can . . . Listen to me, Vicke, do you remember the song
about the pretty little fish? . . . in clear water flowing from the
fountain . . . playing with my hoop . . . my mama told me not to
go outside or I'd die right away. . . ." And that's how Vicke had
spent the night. Listening to him, singing to him, answering him,
making his lips into a smile until the wee hours when he slipped
off to sleep. When he could no longer awaken, the smile still
stamped on his little face, she sent for Roberto. Her love came as
quick as . . . "My God, give me strength. I only want to know
why you do these things to little children. You know they are little
angels and do no harm. Why did you take this little boy instead of
me? Punish us, kill us adults, but not them. Why do you do it?
Why have you left me so alone, alone, alone?"

Levario's jokes become more and more gross and drunken.
They filter in through the window as though making fun of the
Our Fathers and the Hail Marys. Like a gas chamber, the hut is
suffocating in bodies, candles, night, nausea. Dizziness. Vicke feels
sick. "My deepest sympathy, no. My deepest sympathy, no. My
deepest sympathy, NO! My deepest sympathy, NO! NO!" The NO
grows larger like two inflated balloons. NO. They slowly grow
larger in Vicke's mind until the balloons cannot fit in the two
rooms. Then they spill out through the window and get even bigger. Finally the thorn of suffering pops them. "Nooooo!" Vicke

begins to cry. Long sobs mixed with NO. Outside the conversation stops to receive Vicke's suffering through the ears, but liquor has already stopped them up. Is that not why they drink on these occasions? Ah, old cowards! Why aren't you men enough like the women? Why can't you take it like they can? Only Levario's dog answers as though he were mindful of the suffering. His howling accompanies the woman.

"Shhht! Shut up, mangy dog!" Levario kicks him. The dog, with his tail between his legs, moves around the drunken men and then lies down again alongside his master. The talking drops in pitch.

"Poor woman, her parents died just two years ago, one right after the other."

"At the time of the long trek to Marfa?"

"Yes, then. I also remember that the kid got real sick. His face was all red from coughing so much."

"What was it?"

"Well, no one knows, but they say he picked it up over there. Others say that he caught something in the mines when he worked there."

"Poor kid. They should never have let him go."

"Poor Vicke, because she's the one who always took care of him."

"They say that Don Benito and Doña Rosa were over to see her earlier."

"Good grief! The Boss?"

"Yes. When he wants to be, the old guy is okay. He's the one who built these rooms for Vicke on his own property."

"Sure. There's no doubt about it. I helped him do it, although at the time he told me it was to store alfalfa bales, but since it didn't work out . . ."

"So, there you are. I heard just the opposite, that he built them for Vicke because he owed something to her dead parents."

"Really? And what was that?"

"No one knows, but I believe that there's something to it, because when the soldiers came, they didn't cart her off to El Paso. I mean, only to Marfa, but then Ben went over and brought her and Chentito back."

"Well, who knows what the deal is, but if they came to see her, there must be something . . ."

Thus the night fills with life, while inside the remains of death beat against people's breasts. They jab, wounding like a pin. Vicke dozes off from being so worn out, and she dreams nightmares. A luminous little point that turns into an indecisive bat. Then it drops down on the wake like a blind comet. Vicke sees it first as tiny, but then it grows larger, more and more and more, then PLOP! It smashes into her forehead. The beating of its wings in her eyes and on her arms makes her tremble. The bat departs. The woman opens her eyes. Levario stumbles in and goes over to Chente's body. "My God, get that drunk out of here, get him home to bed. Make him respect the little angel, for God's sake." The drunk draws near, while the eyes of the women try to stop him but can't. He begins to feel the coffin. With a sensual pleasure he runs his hands over the cloth. No, it isn't the body that moved him to draw near. It's his work, his coffin. He's so fascinated that he forgets that the coffin is mounted on two pails and he leans against it. The body moves to one side. The man attempts to stop it, but he's drunk. The two fall to the ground with a dry thud.

"Aaaaaaay! Have pity, don't hit him. It'll hurt him! No! Chentito, my beloved Chentito!"

Roberto, who has just come in, runs to help the women who are helping to resettle the coffin on the pails. Then he takes Levario by the arm and pulls him outside.

"Go on, now, Levario. It's time to go. And don't come back." His tone of voice is that of repressed anger.

"Alll I tttried to do was to touch the coffin. . . ."

"Go on, I told you!"

His wife Virginia comes out mortified, saying over and over again how sorry she is, and takes him home. Meanwhile, inside they are rubbing Vicke's neck with alcohol to calm her. She cries for a few moments and then falls back into the snares of sleep.

THE BURDEN REYES WAS UNDER could be felt among the men. He had just come from the wake for Chente. A "Good evening, fellows" and then silence. Rufino, alias "the Cricket," goes up to him.

"What's going on, Chief? You look like the one who's dead."

"Well, what do you expect, buddy? But it's not because there's one little angel more, but because I can't make any rhyme or reason out of this life."

"Come off it, Chief. Look, here's your favorite song."

"Well, let's hear it."

The Singing Cricket wasn't about to get any prize for this song either, but the ballad of Joaquín Murrieta wasn't half bad when accompanied by a well-tuned guitar.

"Gentlemen, I'm Mexican, but I understand English. I learned it from my brother, backwards and forwards, and I can make any American tremble at my feet. I came . . ." Reyes is no longer listening. Reyes's mind expands and overflows his rancor. The kid who had just died is nothing but another in the line of ignoble deaths that include his brother Jesús. For . . .

". . . songs I have sung, punishing Americans, and for the noble and simple Indian. . . ." (Bitch of a life that doesn't even respect the innocent. But I won't leave without making them pay dearly.) "When I was still a child, they left me an orphan, with no one to give me any love, and they killed my brother . . ." (. . . And as long as there is injustice and I see old people mistreated, I will go on, by God, I will go on . . .) "My destiny is now no other, watch out, neighbor. . . ."

"WATCH OUT, BUDDY, don't let your mind wander."

"Eh? Hell, I was just about to doze off."

"Don't tell me you want to miss out on this one."

"Who said anything about fear? It's just my age, friend. You might say I carried you away in diapers, don't you remember? Right from the bridge. Shit, what a struggle you put up. But just look at where you are now."

"What do you expect, man? In those days, I didn't even know where chickens laid their eggs. But now that I see things up close, it's hard to take, you know? It makes your soul steam."

"If they come, we'll just have to scare them. So they'll know who we are. But we'd better not let things get out of hand like that other one did. He really gritted his teeth."

"Well, I guess it's about time for us to go on over. From here we'll go by foot, so watch the horses. And wait until Cricket starts to sing."

THE TEN RANCHERS, following Lorenzo, also dismount about ten yards from the poplar. Then, under the command of their chief,

Chester, they suddenly grab Lorenzo and put a handkerchief over his mouth, tying his hands to his saddlehorn. Then they tie his horse, along with the others, to a wooden stake nailed on the corner of the pump. They keep under cover until they reach the poplar, and once there, they fire into the air first and then the ten spread out among the ditches after the people.

The Cricket sings. You can soon hear the sounds of splashes in the water. Reyes and his men cross the river as if it were something natural. They get to the tree unfazed and unhurried, where they calmly listen to the dry kicks to the body of the one who ran away backwards. *Umph. Umph.* The riders remain passive in the face of his struggling. And then . . . "Waaaaater, fellows!" Cricket yells, and then the firing starts. The men don't shoot to kill, but the surprise makes Ben's henchmen run off scared, leaving the work unfinished. That's what Reyes wants. Then his men take out their whips and chase after Chester and his band, beating them until they collapse exhausted.

Lorenzo, meanwhile, has managed to goad the horse with his spurs until he succeeds in breaking the reins. But he doesn't want it to gallop because his hands are still tied. He makes a great effort to speak, to beg them to have pity, but he can't because of the gag. He manages to loosen the knot on his hands, but Rufino discovers him, and he just manages to apply the spurs when the latter comes up alongside and knocks him to the ground. Then he rolls him downhill and plunges him into the water without realizing the man isn't saying anything. He dunks him once, twice, three times. His body is limp. Rufino finally leaves him lying there and goes to attend those who have been beaten.

"Hey, Manuel, what you got there?"

"Old man Rentería. He still hasn't come to from the thrashing."

"Well, try pouring some water on him."

One by one the pickers huddle together under the fat poplar, some not so worked over as the old man, others with only their mouths open. Reyes goes over to where someone is lying moaning in the irrigation ditch. He discovers a boy shivering. He holds his hand out to him. It looks like the boy is winking at him, but the bruise is too purple for it to be a joke.

"Just look at the beating you got. Come up here. And now you'll know next time not to think it's so great. Don't think for a minute you're going to get paid for your work or the beating. Here, dummy. Take this money and . . . try to earn it some other way."

They went over to where Lorenzo was, just where they'd left him on the sand, on his stomach. Rufino rolls him over himself. . . .

"Listen, chief, I think we went too far with this one. Hell and damnation, it's Lorenzo, buddy."

"Well, nothing's to be done. May God take him and forgive us, buddy."

THERE, NEAR PRESIDIO, the fort rises up at the place they call the Barren Hillside like a crumbling castle. It is an adobe castle without doors that the wind uses like a clay whistle, and there is always someone who goes by at night there with his hair on end and insists the castle is haunted. There are spirits and there are devils that roam from room to room. The unbelievers deny it, saying that it's a bunch of lies, but what is certain is that you can feel history. The legends of the people are the pages of a book that have been torn out and cast on the pyre. . . .

COME ON, FELLOWS, let's hear it for Don Benito, the guy with the goat's beard. Come on, everybody. . . . Don Beniiito, Don Beniiito, Don Beniiito, let Don Beniiito sing, let him yell, Don Beniiito, let Don Beniiito laugh! . . ."

"And where'd you get the idea to cheer him?"

"Because yesterday I saw him walk by with his dandy's clothes on, with one paw on the ground and the other one touching the white beard on his chest."

"He's got a lot of personality."

"No, the little old goat of Presidio's got money and guts."

"Once more, fellows, Don Beniiito, Don Beniiito, Don Benito, the one who owns the store . . ."

"Don Beniiito!"

"Don Benito, the one in the graffiti in . . ."

"Don Beniiito!"

"In the restrooms, on the walls in the streets, on the bankers' checks, on the backs of the cattle . . ."

"Don Beniiito!"

"In heaven and hell, on the lands of Vicke's parents who lost in the county court . . ."

"Don Beniiito!"

"On the parchments, Don Benito the landowner, Don Benito the soldier . . ."

"Don Beniiito!"

"May he be praised, let's all the dead say it."

"May he be praised!"

"For his works and his property, for freeing us from the Man."

". . ."

"Yesterday I remembered I saw him go by with his chest so puffed out that I got the idea to give him a scare. No, I wanted to give him a thrashing if I could have, but the old man couldn't take it, may God remember him when he dies."

"Hold on. Let's all raise our hands and pray for him before he joins us in the fort."

"No, let's give him another scare, for his cleverness with the poor, for his thievery, and for his killings."

"Stop! Be quiet, for the love of God. I can't stand so much name-calling. He was young, he didn't know any better. He was a military man. There was war, people were afraid, there was conflict between governments, he was only an employee. Back then in '63 they told him, come on over here, boy, where the mighty river twists and turns."

"Eeny-meeny-miny-mo . . ."

"And Captain Gray told him, all the cats are black, watch the river from this side, cross over if you need to."

"The troop passed through here and went on toward Chihuahua. Don Benito returned with a soldier's glory."

"Let's hear it, fellows! Don Benito went to war . . ."

"Riding on a bitch, the bitch dirtied itself, and Benito licked it clean."

"And then he got in among us, he conquered lands, he set up a store, he gave everybody jobs."

"Shut up, loud-mouths. We all share in the blame. How many times have I told you to demand your rights and watch out for the wolves and protect your papers?"

"What did we know about the American government?"

"Okay, but why didn't we band together in those days? Why? . . . Go on and see if you jerks can figure out why. When the treaty was written, land rights were assured in writing. Then claims were made, a

lot of claims, to the federal committee. What happened? Of over a
thousand, seventy were approved. The rest were paid for at a dollar-
fifty an acre. Call that justice? Bunch of assholes . . .''

"And you, Don Rubén, what happened to your claim?"

"No, well, death came to me very soon, and just what I thought
happened. My poor old woman, what was she to do? With a
long-barreled pistol she put up a fight, but she went mad, or better,
started to. May God forgive that traitor Lorenzo who also cheated her.
I don't know what kind of deal they made, but there in the courthouse
Lorenzo convinced her to sign over to him. Couldn't do anything. The
dumb broad signed, and after a while she's no longer the owner, but the
government is going to pay her for everything they've taken away. But
let's drop the subject. It wasn't her fault, and I probably would've done
the same thing. . . .''

"I remember her. When I came to these parts, I worked for her."

"And what are you doing here?"

"Well, sir, I came to seek the life I couldn't find on the other side."

"Where are you from?"

"I'm Melchor from Michoacán, sir. I come from far away. They
told me that life was better in these parts."

"But you're real young. How did . . .?"

"Well, sir, I died in a fire here at the fort. I never thought I
would die so soon. I begged and begged the Virgin for her to let me see
my mother, but as you can see, sir, that wasn't possible. I wanted to
show her I had learned to write and that she should be proud of me."

"And what's that piece of paper burned around the corners you're
carrying, Melchor?"

"Just look, sir, it's a poem for my mama that I didn't send her.
When they burned me, I put it in my mouth because it was the only
part of my life worth anything."

"Read it, Melchor."

"Ah, sir, you'll just laugh."

"No, man, why would I laugh? Read it, read it. Right, fellows?"

"Have Melchor read his poem! Have Melchor read his poem! Have
Melchor read his poem!"

"See, man? You have an audience. Come on. And please hold your
head up just as if your mother were listening to you."

"Okay, here it is. It's called Saintly Mother:

You who in your misery made every effort to console me
and to give me the thrashing I deserved,
you who lighted two candles to the saint there in Igualapa
When I fled far, far away from you,
you who are and were very good and long-suffering,
Accept my thanks and my love,
for I can't give you anything but this bunch
of fresh-cut flowers, some from the fields
and the freshest ones from the floating gardens,
Accept them, sweet, good little mother,
Accept them, pretty, saintly little mother,
may God bless you today on your saint's day.
Oh, do you remember all of my bad deeds?
Well, you know they weren't on purpose.
Maybe it's out of longing,
Maybe it's out of trust,
Because I carry your name in my heart
Like your sacred little soul of lilies
Pretty little mother, good little mother, saintly little mother.
You've been good all your life,
You've shed tears for all my sins.
Now on your saint's day all I can give you
is this bunch of freshly cut little flowers
some from the fields and the freshest
from the floating gardens
Accept them, sweet, good little mother
Accept them, pretty, saintly little mother
and hug me tight, bless me a lot
for my spirit sings to you on your saint's day. . . ."

"Long live Melchor!"

"Looong may he live! Now have the Indian Melchor sing. Have him sing! A cheer, fellows . . ."

"Have him sing! Have him sing, have him sing, have Melchor sing! Have Melchor sing, have Melchor sing . . .!"

"*Tzitzi, curapi, tzan en an tzetzas et tzana por su me cuaria . . . ca que tzan tzin, por tunque lo ña miri curiñaaa . . .* cinnamon flower, I sigh and sigh because I remember youuu . . . I sigh and sigh because I remember youuu, *aza guera, aza sentí . . .* because I remember you. . . ."

"Another! Another! Another!"

"Ay, ay, ay, ay, tlazita mutzi caraquia, itzle cuicho, itzla cochitl, aim pero ro quimooo . . . tzama ri cuaria, maqui ni qui ni quia, matzen flor azul, matze pere tzaratzin, male ña quim pa ña quiii . . . ay, ay, ay, ay . . ."

"What're they saying, sir?"

"That they're singing."

"Ah, yes . . ." (The languages become mixed together, become mutilated like pieces of the soul.) "A pretty song . . ." (Other languages are drilled into you like with the point of a pencil and then they turn the pencil around to erase your own as easily as though the soul were written on the piece of paper. Then the language stretches out like a cord and wraps itself around your body, turning you into a ball just like what happened to the cat.)

"Why so serious, young man?"

"For no reason at all. I was just thinking . . . (that justice is a tongue stretched out like a long thread that life grasps onto and ties into knots).

"Why do you wear that cap on your chest?"

"Just out of habit. I tried to stop the blood I was losing."

"Was it a fight?"

"No, it was a bullet that they fired at me when I was running."

"Were you a wetback?"

"No, sir. It was when things got rough back in 1930. Do you remember when everybody was starving to death?"

"Of course I remember. I was in Los Angeles in those days. They said we were making things worse, and they began to throw us out in droves. I remember that in August of that year, it came out in the newspapers that they had thrown 82,000 out. But the funny thing is that they realized too late that we were the only ones who were not asking for help or for food. Things were really mixed up in those days. The immigration service got involved in things without authorization, and they began to make a sweep of people. I remember poor old Anselmo, how he cried because they yanked him out of the house where he'd lived for more than fifty years. But that's all a long story. Tell me, boy, about what happened to you, but first take that cap away from your chest. It looks like you're begging forgiveness. . . . Ah, shit! What a hole! I can see why you keep it covered. Come on, tell me."

"Well, what happened is that my parents emigrated when I was six years old. My papa found work on young Ben's ranch, which had previously belonged to his father, and he considered himself happy, although I had to help him out after school. Life went on like that until 1931, just like you said. The government got the idea that we were a nuisance, although they said they were throwing us out because they felt sorry for us. What they didn't want to understand was that it was worse over there. One day they showed up at home and examined our papers. My papa had emigrated with his papers all in order, but they told him that I was illegal and that I would have to go back to the country where I was born, Mexico. And if I didn't, the whole family would have to return. My mama begged and cried, and my father complained, but it was of no use. And I liked school so much. Well, in any event, I went to live with my grandparents, but I couldn't stand it. After six weeks, and despite my grandmother's warning, I got up real early to cross the river. (Grandma, I'm going over to the other side. No, child, don't cross the river. The field on both sides is dry. Don't cross. Can't you see the spiders are weaving a web to catch you under the water? Can't you see the green chiggers will get into your bones?) It was still dark, but trembling with fear and all alone, I dived in. . . . (Heavy shadows, like dying fish . . . splashing in the water . . . tracks that sink away.) My grandma didn't want to let me come, and as I walked along the road I seemed to hear her telling me to turn back. . . . (Green shadows, your pupils the color of the sea . . . the weeping willow is crying bitter tears for you . . . turn baaaaack!) But I crossed over anyway, like an echo in the mountains. It seemed like everything was against me, because I no sooner was on the other side when it started to get darker and to lightning. . . . (My eyes clouded over with gray clouds and a black sky . . . the earth trembled under my feet, the sky broke into pieces, luminous machete blows.) Then I really got scared, because if it rained I wasn't going to be able to go on, and I think it was fright that made me keep going, even though I knew that I couldn't protect myself if the rain caught me in the middle and I lost my way. And that's what happened. The rain caught me when I was only halfway across the field . . . (pelting my face, whiplashes on my back. Run! Take cover! Turn baaaack!) and the worst part is that it soon turned to hail and I began to be covered with bruises. (Tears, rain, icy ammunition. Have mercy!) My cap was useless, and like a madman I started to run while I cried. I don't even remember how I found the tree (under the sad weeping willow I shivered while the drops falling on the leaves of the plants applauded). I made my body into a ball and cried for a long time until I fell asleep. In the morning I started to walk again, but my heart was heavy, as if the whole world were making fun of me. And when I got there, I cried in my mother's arms like a child. (And you, Mama, you gave shape to time fathoming the transparency of the sea. You liked to gather the waters of the lagoons and rivers in your round pupils. And although the rivers no longer flowed as before, you mended with the rocking of your chair. Don't you remember how I tickled your ribs, and that's how you filled the arroyos of your skin? A laughter of multiform water overflowing your linen petticoats. Life without measure. Teeming seas. A transparent sky that cuddles in your lap.)"

"I can see all that. But, then, how did they shoot you if it didn't happen then?"

"Ah, that was later when I started working, since I was no longer going to school. I was all alone in the fields cleaning up when the patrol appeared. The same ones. I believe that if it had not been for this hate, they wouldn't have recognized me. The fact is that they immediately came over to me. I just asked them to at least let me get my clothes and say goodbye. Well, they said fine, and tossed me into the car. They took me to my home, and they waited for me in the car till I took care of my business, and even though my parents raised a ruckus, it was no good. When I came out, I noticed that one of the patrolmen was drinking some water from one of the faucets a little ways off. The other seemed to be sitting in the car dozing. I don't know what came over me, but I got the idea to run, knowing that I couldn't get away. The one drinking water saw me and fired his gun to scare me. But then he started to run, and when he saw he wasn't going to catch me, he steadied himself so as not to miss. And like a fool I turned around to face him, and suddenly I felt the cold next to my heart. But I didn't feel any pain, just a huge surprise. I remember that I acted scared because when the two came to put the handcuffs on me, I held my joined hands out to them. Then, handcuffed, I picked my hat up and put it over my heart. They helped me get up and I walked with them to the car, but my legs said no. I think that my hat tried to cover the hole my life was flowing out of. But how can a hat hold on to your life? All of us who are going to die are funny, don't you think so?"

"That's for sure. But what are you doing here? You're not from Presidio."

"I'm from the world, sir. Like death. What does it matter if you're from here or from there? Ignorance is enormous, and it's all the same. Poverty, too. The reality is the hole I have here, sir."

"I am reality, gentlemen."

"And who are you?"

"I am Jesús of the river, I am of the water."

"You're nuts, you're of the earth like all of us."

"Of neither ashes nor of clay. I lived in the water, and I died in the water. I am all water."

"And why are you in the fort if you're made of water?"

"Because the fort is made of glass. It's an aquarium."

"Sure, right, nutball. An aquarium with doors of crumbling adobe. You're ridiculous."

"No, the doors are made of voices."

"Ours?"

"No, the devil's."

"That's not true, they're ours. They're cries, the whistling of men who want to cross the river. They are speaking to you, Jesús."

"No, they're the sirens of the sea. They love me, which is why they call to me."

"Yes, they want you. Dead."

"No, they want me to tell them fairy tales."

"Just your old stories, Jesús. What are they going to want your idiocies for?"

"Because my stories are the truth. I am also a siren."

"How so, Jesús?"

"Because my body is in Presidio, but my soul is in the river."

"Didn't it go to heaven?"

"No, because it's dried out on me, and I want to go on living."

"In a hell like this one?"

"Yes, to smother the flames."

"But how, just tell me, are you going to do that if you're dead?"

"I am going to rise again. I will call myself Joseph."

"Your son?"

"No, my brother Reyes's son, and I'm already singing, gentlemen: 'My pride is to have been born in the humblest barrio . . . (this guy's a *real nut. I hope he shuts up fast) . . . the day the people let me down is the day I'll die.' "*

THE FEW TOURISTS who by chance filter into Presidio looking for old things are lucky enough to find a blond relic named Mack. He's assumed to be the expert on the history of Presidio, the fort, and Ben Lynch. So that by the time they leave Nancy's Café, they know all about the number of hangings and fuckings and all those things human beings are capable of. The rest is easy. For a few dollars he'll organize an excursion to the fort. And there he makes them form a semicircle before going in so that . . . But better let the old fart tell it himself. . . .

"YES SIREE, OLD BEN came to this part of the country from his dad's in Alabama. Guess he got tired of driving them dark folks over there and so headed fer San Antone. Ben was still young then, and I guess them wild hairs of his stood up when he heard 'bout the trouble with Mexicans. The story 'bout the slaughter at the Alamo made him mad aplenty. Now I ain't sure when he get to San Antone, but I know he arrive too late. Musta been a sight when he ride into town. You should see a picture of him, here, see? Big, and tall in the saddle, with all that fair hair abristling in the wind. Anyway, he got there a day after all this happened and he sure got burnt up when he hear about Crockett and Bowie died. Couldn't do nothing about, though, just get mad over the whole mess. He wasn't received good either by Mrs. Caulder because she got a patio full of dead, stinking . . . bodies, so she give him a piece of her mind, thinking he had took part in the killing. But he told her different and help her get rid of most of the carcasses. Young Ben was a hell of a cowpoke. He was pretty happy-go-lucky kid them years, but I ain't saying he had no sense in him. He was hard-working and never give his boss reason to talk. He was a tough hombre those years; sure he could sing and yodel, but people wasn't going to mistake him for no sissy. He could fight damned near anybody and boy, could he ride. He could ride broncs till they spilt over, tired as hell. And them bulls, you would think he was born on 'em. But his rough and tough ways don't mean he wasn't brought up right. Hell, no. His folks reared

him good. They tell him 'bout the Lord, and the right living, and
all that 'bout being a loyal and proud man. Sure he was ornery—a
few fights once in a while, but who ain't when you're that age?
And 'specially when you come to a town of . . . people with different folkways and no care fer law and order. I mean, you know,
he come to San Antone fer that there reason. He learned pretty
quick how to deal with 'em in the canteenas and he wouldn't let
no man beat 'im. And he already know 'bout how conniving these
critters can be with knife and all, you know what I mean. Fact, I
heard the reason there ain't no Indians in this part of the country
no more is cause these folks beat 'em at their own game. The first
time he fight, he fight five of them at once and he licked 'em
clean. And when he whipped 'em pretty good, that's when he got
his reputation. He didn't need no gun; the bastards would disappear like shitflies . . . pardon the expression . . . and after that
they would turn yellow and run. Oh yeah, they knew what he
stood fer. Anyway, guess it was about that time that things started
getting pretty stinky down the Rio Grand and they start organiz-
ing the Texas brigade and other lawful organizations to clear up
the mess. You know, horse stealing, cattle rustling, killing white
folks. People nowadays don't pay much attention to the service
these constabulary, Texas rangers they call 'em, give to their
country. Remember, there wasn't no law to protect the citizenry,
so they take it in their own hands. Sometimes when there wasn't
no courthouse judge around, a noose on a tree was enough fer
'em. Hell, with all these desperados running wild, they had to do
something, hoosegow or no hoosegow. Sure, they made some mis-
takes, but hanging innocent people was rare. And although they
crossed the border and followed them outlaws clear to hell, there
was not enough of them to clear up the mess. Anyway, to make a
long story short, the rangers went recruitin' by way of San Antone and they hear of Ben's reputation soon enough. In fact, they
found that the only bad habit he had was seeñoritas and tobacco
chewing, so they hired him. But first they talk to his boss directly
and of course there wasn't no problem. Mixin' with them don't
spoil 'im. So he pack his saddlebags with dried beef and off he
goes (come a ti i yippi yippi yea, come a ti yi yippi yippi yea, 'tis
cloudy in the west and looks like rain and my old slicker's in the
wagon again . . . on a ten-dollar horse and a forty-dollar sad-

dle . . .) I ain't sure what good he done over the Valley by the
Rio Grand, but next thing, he show up in Presidio. It was about
the time the government start getting pretty worried about border
troubles so they start moving soldiers up and down the river. Ha,
ha, but I cain't figure why they sent soldiers to Presidio 'cause it
was just a poor Mexican settlement and there was no white folks
yet. All they find was poor people and a few savages, Jumanos,
they call them. They say the name's Mexican, which means humans, and I guess that's true, hee, 'cause they sure as hell didn't
cause no trouble. That's funny. Sometimes you cain't tell the dif-
ference between Mexicans and Indians. They mix up pretty good,
ha, and they sent the whole company to fight and there was none
to fight. Truth is, they only find a forteen built of adobe by Spanish soldiers, long time before, and it look like it never been used;
yeah, this one here you're seeing. They say it was a custom to
build them everywhere they went, just like the Alamo in San Antone, but this one here wasn't no beauty. Sure doesn't look like it
can even hold water out . . . fact, you probably could blow at it
and it'd fall. Anyway, they find themselves this Presidio del Norte
with nothing to do, so they move up to Marfa sixty miles away
where there was white folks already. But Ben stayed 'cause he was
smart. He know what he was doing but, you know, this is where
the story become different. I mean, Ben was different. He
changed, no doubt about it, 'cause he married a seeñorita. By this
time he was pretty savvy in the language and took to marrying.
Of course, she was different too, educated, pretty, clean—you
know what I mean. But I ain't saying he was a turncoat, though.
He still loved law and order. He always done good like he used to.
He never quit being a ranger, either, and he could run anybody
out of town that give him reason to. One night when he was
acourting Rosary, he got pistol-whipped pretty bad by his brothers,
but he got even soon enough. But that's what I mean, he become
different 'cause he didn't hold no grudge. He learn how to love
these people. I guess that's what love does to you, get soft in the
guts. Anyway, he was a well-respected feller by the community,
and of course they couldn't help it 'cause he was kind to them. He
gave 'em work and food, everything, and of course they look up to
him like a daddy. He learned how to handle 'em and I say this
'cause next thing, he own a hell of a lot of farmland and long-

horns. Fact, he even take over the forteen and use it as a office once his business went good and the soldiers had move out. He started using a lot of Mexican help and from here he would pay 'em with all them wads of bills. Yup, Ben was a good old critter with a big heart; you have to admire a guy like him. Sh—hell, he even made a big barbacoas and invite the whole lot of them to eat. He was fair if they do the job, but if they fail or trick him, boy, he would turn meaner than a . . . angry mama bear. It ain't no bu—lie, either. But people remember more than good deeds. For example, he never forget Paz, the old lady that sell him the land. He done a lot of favors fer her, and even after she died, he took in her daughter Vicke once she lost her husband. Anyway, people remember old Ben Lynch. He was hard-working, kind, law-abiding, etcetera, and all them qualities that an hombre should have. And I ain't saying all about him is true, though. But damned near all of it . . . Okay, folks, let's go in . . ."

"My dad Francisco worked in Ojinaga on a farm, sharecropped, and he raised a lot of wheat. We were no longer needy because my mother worked making tortillas and took in washing to feed those of us who were little. Then he got this field and we were no longer hungry. He raised beans, squash, and lentils, and he put everything aside. When we joined him, it hadn't been long since he'd picked the corn, some huge ears, and he put it in a large trough there next to the house. He made a large bunker with poles to store the corn. We left quite a bit behind when Pancho Villa came. We couldn't take any of it. We came here because Pancho's horses ate it all. A terrible loss. We left the odds and ends we had, our sandals (we didn't have shoes), our beds, everything got left behind. All we came with was a burro, with a wheelbarrow, and a large pan filled with bread dough. That's what we took with us, and we came here to the fields to make tortillas, where everybody camped out. We also brought a skillet and a frying pan and some spoons, that's all.

"The burro walked on ahead with our belongings, with us behind. By the time we got to the riverbank, the water was way up on us because the river had risen. All those who knew how to swim went on, and those who didn't stayed behind over there. Lord, what a mess it was that afternoon. Carmen Chávez's brother came along with another man when the heavy shooting began in the town. They made a raft without really knowing how to. They made the raft to cross the river, but they drowned. Yes, it was sure a terrible mess. We got across because our house was up on the hilltop. All you had to do was to descend the hill, and there was the river. A lot of people crossed over and camped in the woods. People crossed at different points. People scattered, and we ended up in the village of Puerto Rico to live."

"WHEN THE 1910 REVOLUTION broke out, the soldiers would grab people and put them in the army, so almost everybody living in Ojinaga went over to the other side. And since we were out of work, we were nothing but vagrants, as they say. Things were a bit rough, so we survived by fishing. The river was real low, the water very clear and clean, and where there were deep parts we would go with sticks and make noise so the fish would come out and we could spear them with the sticks. The day they grabbed us that's what we were doing.

    "We had come in the morning, me, my little brother, who was this high, Francisco Brito, my cousin, and Chamalía Heredia, who was my uncle. We fanned out into the river, and with our sticks we were scaring the fish. My uncle didn't go in, but stayed up on the cliff, since from there he could see whether the fish came out or not. The water was very clear, and he would tell us whether they were coming up. And after a little bit we could hear the sound of the horses over there toward Quivira. It was an advance party going from Ojinaga to where they were fighting in Mulato. Then Chamalía asked us if he should speak to them, but I told him no because the way the revolution was going, who knows what they might do to us. Well, he did speak to them. He yelled to them, and they rode on over. No sooner had they gotten there than, with their rifles in their hands, they grabbed Chamalía. Then they told us to get out of the water, but we headed for the other side (it really bothered me, for example, that I couldn't go and that they took my brother along, as little as he was. He was really a small fry) but they fired after us. We had to get out of the water, and they tied us up right away. They treated us real bad. They told us that we were Madero supporters and that we were passing supplies to the Maderistas. Eduardo Salinas, who was their chief, ordered them to tie us up with the ropes from the horses. They hobbled us and put us barefoot in the mesquite trees. Then he said they were going to shoot us. There was a cemetery there in Quivira on the top of a hill, and he ordered them to take us up the hill in order to kill us there. They accused us of something we couldn't even understand. Sure, we knew about the revolution, but we weren't involved. Well, they took us there, and all except two of them left for Mulato. They stayed behind with us on the hill. It was real hot and we were barefoot, the whole bit. Well, they concurred and got my brother, since he was the littlest, to give us his clothes and then they dressed us there on the hill. Although they had the order to kill us, they didn't, and one of them did something for us that was real nice. Because, you see, all of us kids would get together on the other side at night and have mock battles. Some from Loma Pelona and others from Terronal. We'd set palm fronds on fire so we could fight each other with lighted torches. Some were Maderistas and others were government troops. That night the Maderista boys named me their captain. Then we used a piece of paper to write out checks to pay the soldiers, and since I was the chief, it was only natural that I had all those papers in the pocket of my pants. They had amounts written on them when we were grabbed.

"I can truly see why God is very great. I was really worried then, but there was no way out. The soldier who went for the clothes frisked me and took everything out of my pockets. But he didn't show it to anyone, for if he had, I wouldn't be here telling about it. Just imagine what would have happened to me. Oh, Lord! But I didn't say a thing, just pretended I was mad and ran away from them. Well, they sent us to Ojinaga, and as soon as the women and soldiers saw us prisoners they started to say all sorts of things to us. Then they let go of us and tossed us in the jail, and we slept there that night. They held us the next day, too. About that time, my grandfather Cleto Heredia, who was sheriff of Presidio County, realized they were shooting at us from the other side and brought pressure to bear. So three days later they let us out and even offered us a safe-conduct pass to the other side. Then I said to my uncle Chamalía, 'See how mad they were? Come on, let's go join up with the Maderistas.' And we did. So that's how I got into the revolution.

"When they did Madero in, I went with Villa. I was a soldier until 1915. In 1915 I left and crossed to the other side, but meanwhile always working for the party until 1920, when things were wrapped up. I was involved with Villa in many ways: I carried provisions, clothing, just about everything. I had crops to tend so it wouldn't be noticeable. I was there in the middle of the field, near the river, and there I sowed my crops. I crossed Hipólito, Villa's brother, over to the U.S. He was living in San Antonio, but they kept an eye on him so he couldn't even stay home. And you have to be real careful about the Americans, because all they care about is what is convenient for them. For money or whatever, they're the ones who brought him over to Marfa, when I took him in. He and other generals stayed at my house, and from there I led them on a march to join Villa's men. I worked like that until 1920 when the revolution ended, along with my people, in accord with him, and when we had to go see him, we crossed the river at night. And so we were always going back and forth.

"Villa was a real devil when he took Chihuahua. He was very clever. We attacked, but we weren't able to make our way in that first time. Since it was the capital of the state, all the soldiers were bivouacked there. So, Villa got the idea to give a false alarm. We grabbed the telegraph operator in Villahumada and made him call Juárez, since it was part of Chihuahua, saying that they were asking for troops in Chihuahua. It was a trap because he called Juárez then and they sent some trainloads of soldiers. When they were on their way, we struck and really whipped them. Then Villa called in that he was going to attack Chihuahua, and turned back and attacked Juárez and took it. That was important because it left Chihuahua hemmed in from all sides. The only outlet was through Ojinaga because we only had a handful of men there. By the time the governor realized that, he came with the millionaires and the troops. They all ended up here.

"The few of us that were here wandered the hilltop with cattle, and when we came into Ojinaga we didn't realize the enemy was in town. Except that my brother-in-law Luis Cortez and some other men from Ojinaga came over to the place the workers gathered and told us. They saved our lives.

"A few days later, we met with the people Villa had sent on ahead, about two thousand, and meanwhile the troops in Ojinaga were swarming all over the place. There wasn't enough room for the enemy, and they spread out over the fields and toward Mulato. Well, first we advanced on the troops in Mulato, and we caught them at the entrance to the small canyon. But a lot of them got away to the other side through El Polvo. We intercepted them at the Alamo arroyo, and engaged them in battle. The next afternoon we surrounded Ojinaga, but they were fierce. There was nothing we could do. There were only a few of us, although it was later said that there were eight thousand of them. Well, we attacked three times, but no . . . There were three large holes surrounded by sandbags where everyone was standing. They killed a lot of us. We retreated in defeat. Three days later, Villa arrived with his men, Maclovio Herrera, Rosalío Hernández and others. Well, even with all these people, we couldn't lick them. But Villa was a real devil, and I remember as though it were yesterday how mad he got for having put his men in such a position. And things were real tough. They had chopped down all the poplar trees and put up barbed wire so riders and their horses couldn't get through. He told us right out: don't pay them any heed, fellows. By morning, God willing, by this very hour, we'll be sitting down to the dinner they're going to fix for us. We have to take them before dinner. No sooner said than done, as it turned out. He gave everyone orders, and they all fanned out on foot. There were a few officers on horseback behind them, but this was for when the attack took place, with the order that anyone who turned back was to be shot. So no one tried to run. But people moved out of sight, and everyone had a sign and countersign. The sign: the exposed body, hatless, the hat here on your chest and the sleeve rolled up, and then the countersign. There were many who got the sign but not the countersign, and those who didn't were killed.

"In any event, it seemed by design that when the sun set, a wind with a lot of dust came up and you couldn't even see your own hand. So by the time the enemy realized what was happening, we were on top of them. And I remember it as though it were today, how we ate their dinner. Let me tell you how that night we set to making coffee with water drawn from a small arroyo nearby. All of us in the barracks drank the coffee, and only the next day did we realize that we had made it from blood. It ran, was still running, because a lot of people had fallen into the large hollow.

When they had run out, a lot of them fell dead and wounded right there. They was a lot of blood flowing, and that's what we used.

"The next morning we woke up to see how many there were and to turn them over. Trucks and wheelbarrows picked up people from the town. They gathered them up and dumped them there where the tank is, the one they call the horseshoe. There was a very deep hollow there, and it was full to the top with the dead. They were carting them off in droves all day long. . . . As you can imagine, the story is a long one. . . ."

Presidio 1942

THE RABBIT, BUNCHED UP into a ball, is sleeping peacefully. He can't imagine why his dream is so pleasant this time. Like a baby's smile, he enjoys the landscape of row after row of lettuce. The rabbit is happy because he's dreaming about eating, crouching down without any worries. Damn! How tough his life is, especially when the humans show up all excited and shooting at him with their rifles. Trucks shining their spotlights looking for his ears, and then suddenly, bang . . . bang . . . bang. Poor brother rabbits. Some are bounty for the dogs, others for the wolves. But tonight the moon rabbit wraps into himself like a happy fetus and dreams. . . .

The moon dresses itself in bitterness and viciousness. It's in a bad mood because it hasn't rained and because the universe is burning in all directions. The Río Grande is only a puddle, the plants are burning up, and the people, burnt-out particles, begin to stick out in the river. The moon hates when it cannot detain them, when there is not enough water to cover their mouths. This is also why the moon is angry. Because the people do not stop their coming and going. That's why it growls.

"Jump! Go on, damn moocher!"

The rabbit's lodgings tremble with the shouting of the moon, and it makes him jump to the ground. Then, startled, he runs off as though he heard the barking of the dogs behind the bushes. Suddenly he feels a slight pain near his tail. He imagines a tiny bullet that moves slowly throughout his whole body like the tickling of a leg that has gone to sleep. He can't get up. He tries to wiggle his head, and it feels as if he doesn't have one. Now, even his eyes feel heavy. Is he dreaming? He half remembers that deep into the night he felt tired and he lay down there by the cave to get his energy back a little bit, but he can't remember when sleep overcame him. And now this strange sensation. The paralysis he felt before has reached his tongue. He tries to look around, but he can only see his body, which is about to burst. The swelling is extreme. He no longer knows what to think, and he doesn't know whether he's still dreaming or if he's out of his mind. Nor is he sure if it was a bullet that he felt on his flank or whether he simply fell so hard from his perch that he hurt his body. Now in the middle of his drowsiness he can barely make out the snake moving toward him with ritual movements. The snake from the low sierra of Santa Cruz closes in on him with his mouth wide open, and he's not certain if the serpent is laughing soundlessly or if he wants to whisper something in his ear. Meanwhile, all his drowsy mind repeats is the story of a small mouse who innocently sat down in front of his hole when a cat appeared with flattering offers of all sorts of delicacies, and then the mouse emerged only to be devou . . . zzzzzzzzzzzzzz.

THERE ARE THINGS that are repeated like dreams, and my father, like so many other men, needs them to make life tolerable. This morning he has awakened dreaming of smiles. He arises from the floor with the same spirit and goes to sit down alongside an enormous belly that seems to spill over from the bed. He contemplates my mama with tenderness, but she doesn't move, not even feeling a mosquito that, sitting on her cheek, insistently draws another mouthful of blood from her. After shooing it away, my papa puts some warped shoes on that sound like the squeaking of the door. When he goes out, he is greeted by soft blows on the leg of his pants. It's Chango's affectionate tail.

The dog doesn't have to hear him say "Come on, let's go see dawn," because he will follow him as he has always done, and the two will walk together to the cotton fields. They will go to the same place where Papa José has taken us to dream so many times, and there he will sit until he's drunk with God. Then his funnel-body will begin to suck up the thousand colors emerging on the horizon. But the magic cloth quickly dissolves, and the clouds will remain completely undressed, prepared to receive the king.

My papa has always believed that the clouds are poor, deceived nymphs. He thinks this because when the sun uncovers its face, it immediately starts to laugh itself crazy. And thus, laughing and laughing, the sun injects him with the energies necessary to live. But the sun also makes fun of him, and the sun's laughter changes into the viciousness of a dog trying to eat its own tail. And Papa only comes back to reality when he realizes he's being roasted alive. Then, shaking his head without being able to believe it, he will speak to Chango: "I won't be like he is, friend. Yes, I would awaken with young bones and I would thank my fortune, but I would not burn, nor mock, nor go mad." Then on the way home, he will walk dreaming about one day living in a similar kingdom and that some day he will sleep in the Creator's house . . . in his own way.

José, after having celebrated the dawn, felt in a good mood and before going to wash his hands, gave a peck to his pregnant beloved, who was making his lunch for him. She answered him with a smile that was a little forced.

"How did my little darling wake up?"

"Fine. . . ."

"Did he give you trouble again?"

Marcela shook her head.

"You just wait and see what comes out. Then you'll forget all this."

"I hope God's listening to you, José. I want him born well."

The woman had good reason to be worried. Three years trying and nothing, until finally she had gotten pregnant. The happiness, nevertheless, had lasted briefly, since she had started to suffer right from the start. And now nine months later, it was late. The old woman Vicke, her mother, was also concerned, which is why she had stopped working in the Rocha house. Now she did the washing and ironing here.

After eating their breakfast in silence, she with a bitter taste in her mouth and he with the good mood he'd felt since Saturday, José gave her another kiss.

"Take good care of yourself, José. Be careful of the sun."

"Don't worry, my old lady." He went out.

THAT MORNING the sun laid bare the chocolate houses with such a great blast that the smoke coming from the stovepipes could not even be made out. That day the people, already scorched, would be set afire by the sun, and they would be ready to call it quits for the week by midday. Little by little the song of the birds turned into a shrill cry of anger: afterwards the cicadas would continue their own song to end up their self-destruction—insects whose bodies were found clutching the bushes.

Cars and trucks could be seen in the distance, full of workers on their way to different parts of the fields. José's buddy Teléforo was doing the same: he went sounding the horn from house to house, picking up those under his command.

Teléforo deposited the cleaners at the section of cotton that was the least dirty, and when they saw how clean the furrows were, their hearts picked up. They quickly bunched at the edge to sharpen their hoes vigorously, and when they heard Teléforo give his son instructions to take charge of the supervision while he went to check on the wetbacks he had working down by the river, they could barely contain their enthusiasm. Chale was a good fellow, and when he wanted to he let them slack off. But now he spoke to them with a serious tone.

"Okay, come on, you heard the boss. No loafing around. Hop to it or I'll report you."

"Whew, the guy's a pain. Come on, let's take his clothes off so he'll stop acting like he's the top cock," Jusito proposed, while the women turned red and quickly scrambled off among the furrows. Smart-aleck kid! Couldn't keep his mouth shut!

Chale, seeing how mad the faces of the others were, burst out laughing.

"What a bunch of shit. You believe me? This kid's not crazy, not by a long shot. Who told you I was a friend of work? Life is short, guys. Take it easy—anyway, you won't get any prizes."

They slowly set to, and after a while all you could see were heads with caps among the cotton fields. They also didn't take long in discovering the trick. Damn creepers were wrapped around the plants so that you couldn't even get across. Just one of those bothersome weeds was enough to make a mess for everyone. Hoes were out of the question. You had to crawl down on the ground and pull the root out by hand. That's how they spent the day, buried in a labyrinth like a drunk who can't find the door to his own house. The bodies showed up on the edge during the breaks, soaked bodies, with spitting faces, coughing, tossing their hoes in the drainage ditch and going over to a nearby tree. Then eternal movements of the head, toward the direction where help was to come—the yellow truck of the old man who brought their wages. But there was nothing to be seen, and then their eyes fixed on the damp female bosoms, as though the best encouragement of the world sprang from there. The feeble old men, by contrast, think about how they'll manage with the check this time, while the women miraculously put new shoes on the kids after having made a calculation of the two- or three-week-old unpaid bills. Damn brats. Their feet are like iron. Farther off, the knot of young men are savoring the cold bath and beers.

THE SCENE IS REPEATED on the bank of the river. With one exception: Leocadio with the pockmarked face is furious. His audience, which normally applauds his creative gifts, is now mocking him because his stories have the tendency to end on too fantastic or stupid a note. Today they have been unable to swallow the true story of the man who was so strong that he could break blocks of sugar on his forehead. That's why he's angry.

"Don't pay any attention to those jackasses, compadre. Go on."

"No, they can go fuck themselves. They all think they're so smart. . . ."

"I told you not to pay any attention. I know you can't be bothered with that stupid book-learning crap."

"Well, you know you're right, compa, because even if we haven't been to school, we know more than all that riffraff, right? Just tell me what you want to know, compa, and let's see if I don't know it."

"Well, I've always wanted to know how we humans got started. I was never clear about that. How did all this business start, compa?"

"Well, now you're about to find out. They say that it was very dark and everything, and God felt very alone and on top of it there was no light. But I believe the real truth was that He didn't have anything to do, and one day just out of curiosity He began to blow just like you do to get the ants all riled up, you know? And then He said, 'Son of a bitch' and stepped back. Because the sun lit up in His face and left Him almost blind. And He really liked what His blowing had produced, so He went on with a moon, and He gave her an earring for decoration. It was turning out just great, know what I mean, compa? Then, all excited, He began with the earth and added water. There's the proof of it, compa, that river running there. Then . . ."

"Stop right there, compa. You're saying He did all this on His own?"

"That's just what I'm saying, as God is holy."

"Listen, His hands must be as big as Lencho's, don't you think so?"

"No siree, He only had to think about it, He puffed a little, and that was it."

"Hot shit! You mean to say He did everything just with His head?"

"Yes."

"So then He really scored big."

"That's right. He said, 'I'm going to think sun,' and poof! There it was, as round and hot as a stud. And the stars? The same thing. But just get this, compa, the best part was yet to come. What do you think was missing?"

"Well, the animals."

"No, man, us. The humans."

"Hold on, just hold on. And what do you think we are, compa? Nothing but damn animals. And if you don't think so, just look at Chango Pérez's face. If he isn't an animal, he's at least part animal."

"No, man, just stop right there. That's another matter. . . . But you're getting ahead of me, compa. Let me go on."

"Go on, then."

"It happens that in those days, the snakes walked on end."

"Shit!"

"Don't get scared, compa, because they didn't bite. And even more so they didn't bite God, because He's the one put them on earth that way, just like I'm telling you. So about that time He thought about making man, but He had a tougher time with him. This time He had to use His hands. He picked up a clump of mud from where the stream watered His garden, and He blew on it. And what do you think came out?"

"A woman."

"No, compa, it was a big macho man, this size, like Samson, and . . ."

"Listen, compa, I think you're mixing things all up on me."

"No, that's how it happened."

"Well, I think you've got it all backwards."

"Calm down, compa. The story's complicated."

"Sorry, a little complicated. But . . . didn't He make woman first?"

"No, I'm getting there. God said, I've got to give this man a companion, and He yanked a rib from him with His hands."

"No, compa, that's starting to sound fishy. You're just making up crap. How the hell . . . ?"

"He didn't even bat an eye. My idea is that He didn't even realize it, because don't you remember that at the beginning all He had to do was blow?"

"Well . . . she seems a little on the noisy side to me, if you want to know what I think."

"And if you think the man He did up was great, you should've seen the woman."

"But it was just the oppos . . ."

"He came up with a hot number like those beautiful daughters Lencho makes. You can imagine, and to make it worse, just think, both of them were stark naked."

"That's fine, if you say so, no problem. But in any event, no matter how I look at it, the thing's a mess. And how were they going to resist you-know-what?"

"I'm getting to it, but don't jump ahead. So God put the two beautiful creatures in that garden they call paradise, where even the devil couldn't get in. But I ain't saying there was no devil, just that God had already warned them. 'And you better be careful you don't listen to him,' He told them, and they obeyed His order."

"And what did they eat there, compa?"

"Ah, God blew them an apple tree."

"And so they spent their time eating apples! Sure!"

"No, not that, because that was a sin, but the leaves were as good and as sweet as the apples themselves."

"And so they spent all their time eating? I thought they fu . . ."

"You don't let me speak, compa. Pipe down and wait until I'm done. Then you can ask me questions."

"Okay, compa, don't get mad. It's just that I'm finding it a little hard to swallow. Go on, don't get mad."

"It turned out that since they were in paradise, they didn't feel anything was missing, like you know . . ."

"Yes, like fucking."

"A real bore. Until along came one of those snakes who said to the woman, 'Eat an apple and you'll see how pretty your cheeks'll get.' And the vain woman . . ."

"But didn't you tell me that it was like she was raised on burro's milk?"

"Yes, but she lacked color. But what's important is that the snake was God's enemy. He was the devil himself. And he went and tempted her."

"Where did he tempt her, buddy?"

"Damn it, compadre. It's impossible to talk seriously with you. Don't act dumb. I want to say that he convinced her to eat an apple. Then God got real mad and threw them out. From then on they had all the things we have, problems, tastes, desires."

"You said they could . . ."

"Yes, then they could. They let themselves go and began to have children."

"You'll have to excuse me, and I know you're going to get mad, but you don't convince me. I don't buy that bit about blaming the snake. That part about blaming the snake, and worse, blaming the woman, that's just too much. How the hell do you think a stud was going to stand it without touching her thing, especially since both of them were stark naked? Excuse me, but I just don't believe it."

"Well, compadre, you can just go to hell. And don't ask me to tell you about anything. If you want to know something, go someplace else. Don't count on me, that's all. I'm gone."

"Wait, compa, don't go off half-cocked. You don't know how to talk like a civilized person. Right away you get all hot under the collar."

"Fuck off, compadre . . ."

QUIET AFTERNOONS. Striped uniforms. They rub their sunburn in the afternoon. The white lines of dried sweat on the shirts smell bad, but that doesn't matter. The people leave them on to eat the first warm meal of the day. The fevered heads eat silently, the slow movements as though they were living an eternal monotony. But then the sun fades, and little by little the bodies come alive again. The young men like Chale and Jusito go off to the pool hall, to the bar, to the movies, over to the other side to spend the last five bucks they have. By contrast, the old folks go off to do their weekly shopping and to pay what's left on what they owe. Then they return home with a six-pack, happy for the fresh air, loosening tongues that have been thick and dry all day. And nearby, behind the mesquites and guame trees, down by the arroyo, out in the field, the kids are running and yelling, feeling life. They play hide-and-seek, tag, London bridge, while elsewhere old voices, husky voices, voices and more voices continue to deny death.

Night falls, a black giant. With its silent footfalls and the desire to strangle someone. The people retreat. The buzzing mosquitos whisper in their ear that it's time to take the chairs in. One by one, patches of light appear as if by magic. The adobe huts cringe and draw into themselves with the night. That's the only way they can resist its weight.

THEY SAY THAT PEDRO, the guy who swallowed feathers, was born with a very big heart and that that's why he had to breathe with his mouth open. It was too big for him, they say, but I think that was only part of the reason. Pedro had been born with his mouth ready to laugh, and the most insignificant thing, the worst joke, would make him burst out laughing. The only time he shut his mouth was when he swallowed feathers. They had hit the ball with its insides coming out high and strong, and Pedro had caught it: with his mouth. And even then he'd laughed. That's why I don't think there was any room in him for tragedy.

Nor can I believe that his heart could just burst. His heart was made for laughing, a liquid laughter that ran down his pants. That's why after school, everyone went to the drugstore for refreshments. They would corner him so he couldn't get up, and then the jokes would begin. After a while, the whole gang would get up with Pedro in the middle, so people wouldn't see him. Because his liquid laughter would already have flowed free. Other times in the street:

"I'll bet you wouldn't dare touch his ass."

"I bet you I would. . . ."

And Pedro would sneak up behind the man real slow. Then he would run off. Peeing his pants laughing.

Tonight the gang shuts down the cantina. But tonight, even though they haven't had enough, no one buys beers. It's very simple. No one's got any money. Not fat Nalgas, who always has money from God knows where, not Chango the gorilla, who's being supported by only heaven knows who, nor dry-skinned Güero, who always has something stashed in his sock. And even then, the town won't accept that it's time to pack it in.

"Tell Louie to get his guitar and we'll go up the hill."

"No, tell him to go get his sister."

"Better yours, you son of a . . ."

"Okay, guys, cool it."

It's Nalgas the magician speaking. They calm down.

"I don't know about you guys, but I'm starving. I need to get a bite."

"Yes, but everything's closed."

"Well, then we've got a problem, right? What do you think?"

Silence. Everybody's waiting for Nalgas's words of wisdom.

"Let's hit the chicken farmer."

Everybody's eyes open a little wider, and the plan is quickly drawn: drop one of them out front of the gringo's chicken pen, enter, and wait with his hand out until a chicken perches on it. That's it, wait like a mummy so they won't get upset, and that's all. You go out, twist its neck, and ready. But who's going? Easy. There are no heroes . . . Later, one by one they turn and look at the car. Feather Gobbler is asleep. As always, with his mouth open.

"Pedro!" Louie yells as loudly as possible. Then, the rest is easy.

"I'm coming," he accepts, half asleep.

They stop quite a ways off, with the motor running. Dogs are barking on all sides. And on all sides people are sleeping as usual. Dead.

Pedro stumbles out of the car. He's quickly swallowed up by the dark. Meanwhile, the wait in the car is worse than Feather Gobbler's risk. The minutes are hours, gunshots, beheadings, death, and finally the silhouette appears with something bulky at its side. They open the door for him and he gets in, breathing hard. Then there's nothing left but the squeal of the tires on the street corner. Everybody holds in his desire to speak until they finally turn into an alley.

"How did it go?"

"Fine, but I could only get one."

Chango feels for it.

"Hey, it's sure big!"

Louie weighs it with his hand.

"Hey, you're right."

Güero holds it up by its feet.

"Son of a bitch, you brought the rooster!"

And in five minutes Pedro spills all the beer in his body. That same night they stuff his mouth with rooster feathers. So he'd pee more, they said. But nobody thought his heart would burst on him.

THE SLURPING OF THE TUBES shakes the body seated on its haunches, and until now he had not felt the weight of his head resting on his chest. Half asleep, Chonito, José's young helper, glances at the running water to make sure he's not dreaming, but he sees the dry ditch. The water must have dried up in the river, he thinks, at the same time he straightens up his body, numb from exhaustion. He can't believe he was asleep for so long, and that the sun didn't even wake him up. A brief shiver runs down his spine, causing him to walk over to the bundle formed by his shirt and hat. Then he picks up the shovel so he can cross over to the other side with the fervent hope that the water in the tilled field is done. But he doesn't have to. José, his boss, comes up.

"What's wrong, Chonito? Are you through?"

"I don't think so, Don José. The pump stopped."

"I know. I've just come from there. When I was walking over here, I couldn't hear it, so I went to see. It started again. I think we'll be done by tomorrow, don't you?"

"Yes, sir, as long as the water doesn't run out."

"I brought you some lunch to hold you until noon and . . ."

"But aren't you going to work over at the old man's?"

"Yes, but I'm going to get that kid Leyva to take care of the irrigation. I'll just fix the dam and the pipes so he'll take care of it. It's not much, really."

"Well, if you want, I'll . . ."

"No, man, the damn migra is all over the place like ants. It's better for you to leave at noon and wait for me on the other side. After they pay me I'll cash the check and pay you."

"Then about what time'll I see you, sir?"

"Wait for me there at the poplar tree around three."

"Okay, boss."

"And be careful because . . ."

"Don't worry, Don José, I know all about it."

"Okay, I'll see you there later."

In a flash José disappears in the sea of cotton by the river, while Chonito sits down again on the edge, this time to put on his misery-laden, warped boots full of pity while he cools his rear on the damp ground. The kid, despite the fact that this is the third night he's gone without sleeping, doesn't try to go fall asleep in some nearby shade. He feels happy because this time his boss is going to win out. He never tires of contemplating the forty acres of plants heavy with fruit. He might wish Sr. José could be here with him to share the precious buds beginning to burst out and kissing the water. But Chonito knows that's a lot to ask for. José, in love with a land that no longer belongs to him, José with his bowed legs must be something more than a sharecropper. That's why he has gone to join the group of cleaners headed by Teléforo.

PRESIDIO—nothing to remember except clouds and the devil. The latter skinny, the former fluffy, both slipping across the sky and making fun of the people, the animals, the plants. It never rains in Presidio, and the boom that emerges from the throat of the clouds only serves to fill the hollow of silence for an instant. But not even the echo from the Santa Cruz sierra is enough to scare the devil. The scoundrel never forgets the town. With a firm hand he squashes the mesquite and the thin brush. With both hands he squeezes the water out of the formerly mighty Río Grande, reducing it to a mirage, a puddle.

But the old goat-foot is not all evil. He has a very long swing mounted on top of the sierra, and now and again he shows up at the fiestas dressed as a dandy. On other occasions he appears in the form of a burro and allows himself to be ridden until the kids, poking around with a stick, discover he has no asshole, and then he disappears, leaving behind the smell of French cologne. Nevertheless, his favorite joke is the cat and mouse playing the hide-and-seek game. The border patrol cat, his face furrowed, waits to pounce on the mouse, whose only defense is the hunger he carries in his stomach. The mouse jumps the puddle and begins the ridiculous flight, while the devil rolls on the ground laughing.

THE SUN DRINKS HIM UP, burns him. The sun is laughing because he's drying him out. The plants, too, feel useless, not knowing what to do, while the thirsty sun drinks everything down to the last drop,

Chonito wants to cry but can't. His throat hurts, even when he's in the water up to his neck. He knows that he shouldn't move because the water will escape, and he's shaking, he's so scared. He moans. Meanwhile, the boy is turning into steam.

He continues in the same position, reliving the incident one more time. It happened so fast. After Don José had left, he had leaned on the shovel, and suddenly sleep overtook him. The jeeps of the immigration officials awoke him, and with his mouth hanging open he saw them searching about without noticing the opening in the irrigation ditch where the water had started to run out. It seemed as though he had never seen that scene, never heard the yell to "go for the riiiver" of the wetbacks and then a bunch of heads rushing toward the river. How many times had he witnessed that spectacle, the kicking ass of old guys and children or an accident like the one last month? The patrol plane had flown very low, right over their heads, *wooosh*. The man on horseback had gotten his head sliced clean off. They say he's still looking for it at night. Or last week when they found the little kid, all bloated and floating in the irrigation ditch. People said the patrolman had only wanted to scare him by ducking him in the water because he was always crossing back and forth.

After all the ruckus had died down, Chonito noticed the water running out, and at first he wasn't worried. But then he got nervous and started shovelling like mad. The water was carrying the earth away, and the hole was getting bigger. He shovelled until his blisters were bleeding and then, since he couldn't think of anything else to do, he took his shoes off and got into the water, jamming his body into the opening. That's how he'd have to stay, waiting for Don José, who would not be long in coming back, for it was already close to one.

His feeling of anguish vanishes when he thinks what a man he is. He can handle everything now, although he's barely twelve years old—the hoe, the shovel, picking, packing, everything. And since he knows he can do things like a grownup, he feels proud of himself. But then he returns to the situation he finds himself in and he feels ashamed. What will Don José say? He had been so dumb. Water is so scarce, and if old man Lynch sees it running out on the road, he'll get mad. What a jerk, I didn't see what was happening.

Now he begins to feel sleepy again because of the fresh water running around his arms, his legs, his neck. The murmur of the water lulls him, but he resists because he feels so strange, like he's floating on air, as though his waiting will never end. Like that time when by accident the tractor had started to roll. He didn't know what to do except to go around and around in circles until it ran out of gas. A drunken eternity went by until he got the idea to ram it into a trailer. Then he had run off to his house. But that time he'd found a solution. Not like now. Now he would have to wait and wait and wait. . . .

José has to shake Chonito hard to get him to come to, and when he finally opens his eyes, he starts crying. Then the boy, all numb, lets himself go on the man's chest. But after José has gotten over his fright, he can't help but smile, and the kid, when he sees him smiling, stops crying and pulls away roughly. Then he runs off toward the river. Meanwhile, gales of laughter strike against him, stopping only when he reaches the banks of the river.

THE DEVIL IS FEELING PLAYFUL, but at the moment the only thing he can think to do is look at his body in the mirror. Standing there naked, he sees he has no sex and no hair. From the front his sex looks like that of a newborn girl. He turns around but can't find his anus. He tries now to think of a simile, a metaphor to describe his beautiful body, but he can't find a "happy comparison." He thinks and thinks, and the only thing that comes to mind is a series of questions. The failure upsets him so much that it puts him in a bad mood, and he looks around for some other way to entertain himself. Immediately, he dons a clown's suit and looks at himself again in the mirror. Bah! That game is too child-ish. It's not worth anything outside. He's got to be more serious about his jokes, and he's got to continue to mock human life.

Now he uses a black brush to accent his pointy eyebrows and then he immediately stretches out his arm to scrape some sky blue. This he rubs in his pupils. As a final touch to the upper part of his body, he puts on a blond wig and a Texas hat. Then he looks for a suit to cover the rest, and finds a dark green one, his favorite. When he's got it on, he grunts his way into some boots to cover his rooster feet. There, he's ready! On the way out he winks at himself in the pool he uses as a mirror. Outside, he climbs on his swing . . . but . . . hold on a moment! He almost forgot! But there's still time. So he doesn't worry about it. He hikes himself up high, high, until he can reach a star. He quickly plucks it and places it where his heart should beat. Ready! The devil is ready to continue his eternal joke.

To GET TO PRESIDIO you have to go along a narrow road of guame and mesquite trees. With the air glued to your eyelashes and a sluggish mind, your body drops away from you and falls into a well that was never completely dug out. Or you slip down a funnel. Before you fall you sit on the top of a hill to see, in the background, goat droppings, houses that look all alone in the vast agricultural terrain. Houses of poorly tended adobe, houses that beg God for mercy. Houses: old shoes abandoned in a sun that shrivels everything. Like a drunk, you let go of the top and then you let yourself slide down a road that divides Presidio in half. Like a rolling wheel, Johnny's Bar, Texaco, Ron's Lumber, Harper's (they bored through Harper's forehead so he'd give up the loot). Phillip's 66, Juárez General Store. Slowly cruising.

"What about the downtown? What about life?"

"Ah, this is Presidio, mister. Don't ask any more questions, because I can't answer them. What about what? Ah, yes. The people are down by the riverbank, among the rushes, under the bridge, on top of the bridge."

"And what's across the border? Mexico?"

"Yes, mister, Ojinaga." (Presidio divided in two by time.)

"Reyes Uranga?"

"The second house, the one with the chicken coop. But he doesn't live there during the day, only at night."

"And the youngster?"

"José? Oh, he's something else again. If he's not at home, go look for him among the cantaloupe, the lettuce, the cotton, under one of the harvesting bags, or leaning over a shovel downing tacos and Kool-Aid. Maybe down at the packing shed. By the way, who are you?"

"George Evans from Marfa. I want to speak to him, understand?"

"Is anything wrong?"

"No, nothing. I just want to talk to him."

"Well, if that's the case, you'll find him among the Santa Fe refrigerator cars playing ball in Jones's packing shed with workers with chapped and sweaty hands and baggy clothes."

"Where?"

"You mean where is he? Well, look, just follow the same road to the outskirts, and there where the cow pens are, that's where Jones's packing shed is."

"Thanks a lot."

"Don't mention it."

(TWELVE HOURS times 50 or 70 cents between 10,000 times 10 minus transportation, minus the cantaloupes eaten, minus those who didn't show up today because they got the heaves and the cramps or they got drunk, minus the advance paid to Carrasco, who didn't come back. He's still a hard-working ole boy. See if I can get 'im to train for shipping orders.)

"Joe! Here's someone to see you."

"He's in the can, Mr. Jones."

"Done something wrong, Mr. . . . ?"

"Evans. No, I just came to talk to him about some incident last night."

"He'll be out in a minute. Hey! Son of a bitch! I told you to step on it, Manuel. The boxes over here. The fellow's getting old, you know? I just keep him around to help 'im out, but we get old sometime, you know? Hey, here he comes."

"Joe Uranga? I'm George Evans from . . ."

"No, sir, I'm Joe Durango. Uranga is not working here."

"Damn it, I thought you said Durango, Mr. Evans. I'm sorry . . ."

"Know where I can find him?"

"Yes, sir. He work with Mr. Lynch at the farm. But he don't go by the name of Joe. They call 'im José."

"What's the dif . . . Oh, well, thank you, and sorry to bother you, Mr. Jones."

"No bother . . . Hey! Son of a . . . more boxes over there!"

THE RAIN IS OUT TO MELT God's house, but it can't. It pecks in vain at the window, and when it grows tired, its tears of anger roll down the wall. Then, accepting defeat, it comes in through the

door that opens now and then and sprays the nearby bodies. But
these holed-up men don't care if they get wet. They're there because they want to be. They're there to take stock of women's legs
and to guess the reason why so-and-so has come so late, as they do
now with Marcela. Everybody looks at her, everybody's thoughts
are on her—the woman who, it seems, has been expecting forever. . . . They don't know if she forgot to make the sign of the
cross when she passed by the holy water or if she refused to. She
merely sits down and begins to wipe her face with a cloth. (I
shouldn't have come. All eyes are on me, they know. Mama was
right when she told me, don't go, but I insisted. Now all I'll be is
a nervous wreck.) "My dear children, have no fear. Set your cares
aside. Let us trust in God, for He knows what He is about." (Yes,
Father, but now the river won't let me cross over. I want to go
with José. I'm very frightened that maybe they're waiting for me
outside and they'll carry me off to the office.) "We know that the
flood can be disastrous for us, but the gospel . . ." (My God, what
am I going to do if they don't let me go home, if they stop me and
ask for José? Dear God, help me . . . .) "And now let us pray,
pray to the Lord that He remove us from danger, that He bestow
on us His blessing. Let us pray. . . ."

The sermon is brief. The priest is just as impatient as the congregation. There is nothing left to say. Everyone knows that their
hopes are bankrupt. Now they all stand, except for Marcela. She
remains seated a little longer because at that moment her legs are
made of rubber and she can no longer move the way she used to.
She now tires a lot. Her feet swell. Her belly is like a swollen river
and makes her feel uncomfortable, now more than usual because
I've been a pest for quite a while now. That's what I think, because she doesn't even make an effort to stand up. I guess I'm
more of a pest now because I have heard people comment that
when I move I hurt her, and I guess now that I'm more developed
and stronger, it will be that much worse. Undoubtedly that's
what's happening at this very moment. I'm cramping her stomach
real bad because that's what happens when I get ideas. I move
around a lot. I don't want to, but just a moment ago I decided to
sharpen the little bit of memory I've got and to bring together
things that have happened so I can write it all down when I'm
born. And the effort to recall and put it in order makes me move,

just as I'm doing now. My poor mother doesn't know about my faculties. She doesn't know that I have a very precise image of her and what's happening outside. She thinks what she has in her stomach can't feel or hear or think. But she's wrong. She's going to get quite a surprise when she sees I'll be able to write the minute I'm born. It's a real drag for me to be stuck in here, to always be floating in something like a liquid, sticky gum. When I stretch, I right away feel my feet and hands hit against a net. I image that that's what flies feel when they try to get free from a spider's web. I also think about my poor mother. How it must hurt her. I wish I were already born. But she insists no, because she thinks it's better for me, and like all mothers, she doesn't want to see her child suffer. Everything for my child, she says. The fact is I feel bad because I know the suffering she's going through out there, and I can't do anything about it. My hands are tied, and at times I don't get angry with her but with what I hear going on and what I imagine. And my mother's just as stubborn as always. That's why she's refused to give birth to me. I don't want my child to suffer, she says, but I think she's protected me enough. Can you imagine what it must be like to carry a child in your womb for so long? I'm tired of . . . Excuse me, Mama. I'm going to make myself a little more comfortable. Ah . . . ay . . . now I hear the little bells. Get down, kneel . . . That's the way . . . I promise now to remain quiet while the priest drinks the blood of God. If the situation is the same as every Sunday, the church'll be full. Just like always. Like a tired picture that shows everything. The priest up front with his gestures. Dressed the same. The same words. We are all sinners, but the meek will go to heaven. You have to suffer in order to inherit eternal life. That's why Christ loved and suffered. He set an example for us, and you've got to follow it. The children who still haven't learned the movements in order and don't know the responses are probably up front. They don't care much. Nearby'll be the beatas dressed in black hanging around the statues and the dripping candles, deep in prayer. All the same. At the other end, just behind, are the humblest, as though it were the practice of centuries. All the same. The picture of the church and its congregation tells it all. The boring picture is repeated when they go to communion. The line on the right will go first, perhaps because they're surer of salvation, while the other line waits. The little bell! The little bell is ringing again! My mama and the others lower their heads when the priest raises the representation of the body in the form of a round piece of bread. I never knew why they do it, I mean, why they lower their heads. Is it by habit or out of respect? Is it because they're afraid of the mystery or because they feel guilty at eating the body of Christ they think they don't deserve? Who knows? I also think that it's ridiculous to feel my mother beat her chest, something I also don't understand. It seems like she wants to punish herself, to strike her heart because it's beating. Maybe she feels guilty to be alive or she's renouncing living? Come on, get up, Mama, wake your limbs up first. Be first just this once. Come on, beat 'em to it. Look, you've got the same right. Truth is it no longer matters to you. But it ought to. Look at that girl. Let me out so I can slap her. Why does she shove in front of you, pushing you to one side? Does she have greater privilege than you do even in God's house? But I shouldn't bother you with my grumblings. I promise to calm down. Now . . . open your mouth . . . that's it, that's the way. Come on, go on back, but don't clasp your hands, please, because I don't want you to fall down like you did last week. Remember, you didn't eat last night."

Marcela returns to her seat on her legs like butter. After the priest has given her the host, he tells her to wait for him because he wants to talk to her. Worried, she goes and kneels in the last row behind a stocky old man, as though that would erase her fear. There, on her knees, she prays and (what if I were to come out right now, quick, without waiting for mass to end? No doubt the priest already knows and wants to ask me about José. Dear God, I can't stand it any more . . .).

Outside, the scattered rain continues its pecking while the congregation gets to its feet. At that moment Marcela notices a tall man, a blond who comes in without removing his Stetson hat, and he goes up front as though he were right at home. Then he comes back with eyes like an eagle that roam from side to side. She feels a strong shudder go through her, but she hides it, arranging her veil. When the man notices her, he momentarily halts in front of her and smiles. Then he winks at her and goes out. She's left stunned, unable to move.

"Now, Mama. Mass is over. Jump now. Why is your heart beating so hard? What? Is it still raining? How are you going to get home? You can't run. . . . Are you going to sit down and wait? But, no, please don't run. Mamaaa. . . ."

BY THE TIME MARCELA reached home, she was all hunched over, her hands clawing at the air. She was screaming for them to get him off her.

"But, who, my daughter?" a little old lady asked her while Chonito's eyes grew wider.

"The devil," the terrified woman howled.

Whispering a Hail Mary, Vicke quickly made the sign of the cross several times on her forehead and began to sprinkle the room with holy water. After she'd done that, she gave her a spoon of sugar water for the fright and succeeded in calming Marcela down enough so she could say what happened.

"As soon as I came out of church, I was struck by a shadow that kept saying it wasn't going to let me get by. And it laughed and laughed like it was crazy."

"It must be your nerves, ma'am," Chonito stammers.

"Yes, Daughter, it's fear."

"I tell you I saw him. He had different shapes. First it looked like he was going back and forth on a swing just like he was going to knock me down every time he swung by. That was when I began to run, and he turned into a ram and kept butting me with his head. When he saw me fall down, he burst out laughing again. Then he disappeared in . . . du . . . Aaaay! Get him off me! Aaaay, he's coming! Please!"

Marcela begins to beat the air with her hands, running from one room to the next. She knocks the table over and breaks the dishes. Then she crashes into everything in her way. The old woman and Chonito trap her on the bed and struggle with her until they subdue her. The woman's hands are all stiff.

"Please help me! Look at my fingers, Vicke! I can't straighten them!"

Marcela attempts to open her fingers herself, but they gnarl with each other. Then she tries to run away again, but the two pin her down while Vicke talks to her, prays over her, makes the sign of the cross over her paralyzed hands and rubs her whole body. Little by little the hysterical woman calms down until she can at last move her fingers. But her gaze is far off. She doesn't answer their questions. Marcela doesn't open her mouth. She just sits there on the bed like a zombie, her paralyzed eyes on the wall. When they've tried everything in vain, they stretch her body out on the bed. Marcela doesn't resist. Vicke and Chonito think that perhaps after she sleeps a little it will go away, but they don't know the woman's eyes will be dilated for the rest of the day.

The devil withdraws to die laughing. Then, all tired out, he lies down on the wet stones to snore at his leisure.

CHONITO GETS UP from the floor where he'd lain down exhausted after crossing the river and goes directly to the vase full of water. After emptying it, he looks blindly for the leak. When he finally hears the tinkle of the water on pewter, he centers it beneath the leak. He immediately takes the cloth and puts it over the vase because otherwise the sound won't let him sleep. This done, he goes over to Marcela's bed to make sure she's all right. Her deep snoring satisfies him. Great! She's finally fallen asleep. He can't even remember. The woman had cried so much. "I started to think we couldn't control her. She was shaking so much. Poor woman. Not even when I assured her that Mr. José was fine and that he was waiting for her did she feel consoled. It's the first time I see her so, so, I don't know how to explain it, but she was all torn to pieces on the inside. They say that women get that way when they are expecting. I hope to God that's true, because if it isn't, this woman is going crazy. I would swear that she already was when I got here. I sure hope she isn't going to go on being sick this way."

"Ah, how I would like to have a chat with you, Chonito. Thank you for everything you've done. Make you understand why my mama is that way. She's carrying one hundred years, just imagine, Chonito, one hundred years of history in her belly. Her sickness is words that can't come out from here, from inside. They stay stuck in the mouth of her stomach until they make her vomit. Night and day she's enduring this sickness, destined never to get used to it. No, Chonito, Mama is not going crazy. She's sick from words she utters like a sigh in ears that don't retain a thing. And then those same words bounce back, going back into her mouth and lodging there. Then they make her throw up.

That's why my mama's crying, and I hope to God that before I'm born they don't poison me, because they also hurt me. I also feel like my mouth is full of pins. I sure hope I get out of here soon, because this bilious silence bothers me very much. Meanwhile, don't let them come in, if you can help it, Chonito. Don't let the poets sing those glorious epics of life. Cut their balls off for me until I'm born. If they speak to you of deeds, beg the dead to applaud and cover them with leprous kisses. If there is love in their verses, sing ballads to them. If they find beauty in Presidio's valley, tell them about the devil and his cave. Show them how he made love to the Indians. If they inspire you with virtue, Chonito, take them up into the hills, when the people seeking miracles leave legs, arms, and eyes made out of metal. Never a whole body. Never a live body. But rest, Chonito; after all, you can't hear me. Some day soon, I will light a match and burn their feet. Some day they will not sleep because the night will weigh heavily on them, like a ball chained to their feet or like a hard rubber ball. The bodies of the tired laborers will writhe in their beds and their bones will crunch. And the dead will invade their minds, will make them cry, will make them laugh, will drive them mad. Yes, Chonito, someday they will not sleep, they will not sleep, they will not sleep. . . ."

The rain has stopped. Inside, the leaks have grown tired of dripping, dripping. The silence is now overwhelming, enormous. Night, like Marcela's body, also seems to have collapsed with exhaustion. Nothing stirs. Not the stars, not the clouds. Not the moon. Nothing. The houses are coated against the night. Leaden numbness and silence. Only a lost breeze runs its cool hands from time to time over the beards of the poplar outside. Then the tree shivers and answers with the soft sound of a tambourine.

Marcela half opens her eyes, but for a moment she can't see a thing. She can only make out the bodies of Chonito and Vicke sleeping in the room. She's lying on her side because it's been a long time since she could lie on her back. The baby she has tried not to give birth to is like carrying a ton of copper in her belly. Beaten into the shape of a sharp cone. She adjusts her eyes a little more to the dark while she thinks about José, José, how he feels, the Río Grande, there's no way over, mass, the priest, it rained, I cried, I slept, what time is it, it must be three o'clock.

She hates getting up at this time, and she'd like to be able to stay there until dawn, but she knows what's waiting for her outside. The mud, the early morning chill, and then the wet wooden bench. She has to go outside, even if it's only an insignificant trickle. The pressure of the child is great. He makes the bed squeak as she sits up and feels for her sandals with her feet, and when she finds them, she puts them on. Then she covers herself up to her head with the blanket and walks toward the door.

"Ma'am?"

"I'll be right back, Chonito, I'm going outside," she answers him with a low voice.

"Marcela, is that you?" the old woman sits up in bed.

"Yes, I'm going to go to the bathroom."

"Do you want me to go with you?"

"No, Mama, I'll be right back." And she goes right out without waiting for the old woman to insist.

The outhouse with its sheet metal siding is not far, but she has to fight the sticky mud that tries to pull her shoes off. She quickly reaches the door, sensing how wet it's going to be inside. The outhouse is a real sieve. She climbs up to the freezing throne, raises her cape, and then sits down, catching a hand under each buttock. All this discomfort for so little. It's just that the child has slipped way down. "At times it seems like its little head is between my legs. But that's okay. There, there he goes . . . moving again. Go on and move, my child, move around because that's the only way I'm sure that you haven't gone and died on me. It doesn't matter that you hurt me. Move around so I won't worry about you. I don't know what's happened to you, but you no longer move like before. I ought to feel you more, what with how far along I am. Go on . . . that's the way . . . that's the way. . . ."

The woman returns and lies down again. The fetus continues to move with soft, serene movements. She enjoys them. She feels happy because there's life there in her belly. "Don't worry, Mama. I know you're not alone. You can't feel me because I don't want to hurt you. It's just that when I get tired of being all balled up as though I were praying, I've got to stretch. But I do it carefully, now that I've discovered that if I stretch my hands first and then my legs, it hurts you less. That's why you can't even feel me, because I no longer have the habit of kicking at you. Now . . . I'm making myself comfortable because you know, the night has been very long and my head fell asleep. My blood is feeling very heavy. I don't know why I fell asleep that way. Perhaps because your heart was beating so hard or because your guts were growling. You know, that happens a lot to you, since you didn't eat yesterday, don't you remember? "How did you fall asleep? You sure gave us all a scare. Your friend came to see you, and Teléforo almost swam across the river to tell my papa, but you calmed down late into the night. It was nothing but nerves. I felt them like tight bonds here inside. Imagine how I felt, with the boom, boom of your heart going hard in my head and your nerves and guts churning like a flood. Those are the times when I suffer the most, because it isn't true that your heart is in your chest, but rather in your guts. It's beating here in my hands, and I'm doing everything possible not to make the slightest movement. Two days ago I discovered that I can move like a compass. If you lie down on your side, I swing into a vertical position in your belly. If you stand up, I go into a horizontal position. If you make movements I don't understand, I float free. That's why you can't feel me, Mama, and I hope you understand. I'm normal and I'm growing fast. You don't know it, but since I began to exercise my mind, I've noticed the development myself. Ever since I started to think about writing when I'm born. And now this disorder doesn't matter to me. The time will come. What's important now is to let everything fly, to loosen your tongue until the time comes. For the first time I'm happy to be able to see so clearly from here, Mother. There's no need to be on the outside, no need even for it to be daytime, because you communicate it to me. Your soul becomes translucent. When you're happy it turns into a white butterfly, and when you suffer, the little butterfly bleeds all over my body. I tried to talk to Chonito tonight to explain your madness to him, but I don't think he heard me. That's something I don't understand. It seems like some people hear me when I think and others don't. I would like to know if they really can see and hear. I don't know why it's only now that it's occurred to me how slow my life has been. I barely realized today that I've stretched myself out like a very fine thread that goes way back; I was with you in your veins since your childhood. And don't forget, you only gave me your womb so I could grow there, but long ago I was a seed bouncing from womb to womb. Imagine existing one hundred years before being born, looking for a place to take root. But rest now, Mama, the night has been long."

AFTER IT STOPPED RAINING, the night got real nice. It was real pretty, with bunches of stars all over the place. Little by little the clouds had slipped away as though they were afraid, leaving a bundle of bright pinpoints. No doubt about it, the sky looked like one of those beautiful cloaks kings drape their skeletons with.

Downtown, all the guys came out of their houses to see what the hell was happening in the silent town. They were all on foot because their old men wouldn't let them use the car. Besides, you need gas to cruise, and everybody was in the same boat without any, like everything else. The damn rain hadn't allowed them to work all week, so some of the fellows had to be happy with rooking around like the Chinaman on the night of the sixteenth of September celebration. Others had gotten to playing craps for a nickel a throw behind Johnny's Bar—after all, you can't even get feeling good with just a dollar. And if you were hot, you could win a pile and then go play pool for beer. But if not, you were out in the cold, as always happened to those who were already as bad off as sleeves on a vest. Usually, the most undeserving asshole would win at the dice. So no matter how much you snapped your fingers and blew on them and treated them like honeys, they always treated you rotten. Not even Little Joe, or Live Jive, or Silver-Eyed Sixto would give you the time of day. They gave you the cold shoulder, even if you tried to talk them up. Shit, it seemed like the dice were loaded.

Other times the guys wouldn't be making asses out of themselves. By this time they'd be over on the Other Side dancing, ogling the girls, the whole story. It was real cool in the ramadas and whorehouses. Gals walking round and round the plaza like a broken record, chewing gum, waiting for you to go over and talk to them. "Say, chick, let's go get a beer over there where the rubber-lip musicians are. Hey, don't cut me off; I'm short already." If you scored, you'd take her and get her a Coke and talk her up. If you were lucky and she liked you, you could put it to her straight: "Say, let's go where it's dark and get it on." If not, then you could just take it slow, dancing with her. In any case, you'd scored and the idea was to take it easy, to play it cool. But now? Can't do anything; the whole thing's an ugly mess. You're forced to spend your time with a foot on the corner, watching the old folks making the rounds, all sad, all of them frightened that the fucking river will piss all over the place. If that happens, then you and they'll all be in a mess. The damn border patrol are also going back and forth as if that were going to stop the river, but their job is all show because there's nothing for them to take care of. Who's going to cross over here with all that water? Besides, it costs an arm and a leg to cross on the barge. Only the guys that come to the dance from over there in Chuco, Kermit and Odesson have enough money to pay the five bucks to Trompas, who played it smart, buying himself a barge and ferrying people from one side to the other. But on this fucking, worthless night, not even those guys can get over. Only the sky's gorgeous. It's either stay home and snooze or hit the boss lady for the buck she's always got stashed away and you split for the show. Don't be stupid and play it on the craps because then you won't even make it to the movies.

Chale, who's been sleeping all afternoon, gets up and goes to the bathroom. He remembers the date he's got with Jusito, and he starts to get ready. There in front of the mirror, he washes the sleep off his face, and then uses the foam to make himself a beard like Santa's. He takes out the razor, and in a few minutes his cheeks are nice and smooth. His gal likes them like that. Then he smears Parrot gel all over his hair and shapes a neat ducktail. As he bends over he notices his shoes are all scuffed, and right away rubs them against the back of his khakis because there's no time for a speedshine. It's already close to eight o'clock, and that dude is probably already waiting with the chicks. So he quickly slips his pants on, leaving his shirt opened on top so he can sport his hairy chest, and he's ready. "I'm not going to eat, boss lady. I'll be back in a while."

Just when he was about to get into his old man's jalopy, he noticed it had a flat, and he got so upset about it he kicked it until his big toe was sore. After he'd sworn at it for the last time, he took off on foot. His anger didn't go away quickly because he was still thinking about the fiestas he'd missed out on, although he knew full well the danger of crossing the river. He recalled the beating Betabel had gotten, but it had been his own fault that he'd gotten knifed because why'd he try and go steal the gal away from that guy out in the open? Yeh, it was all his fault. It's better you can't get over. You'd just better cool your heels here until the heat's off. What's the big deal? You can get it on with Mary, man. Don't be a fucking jerk with her, the dame's got a crush on you, she really loves you. Otherwise, how come she's put up with so much? But the guy'd counted on the car to get out of having to take her to the movies because he was flat broke. The only buck he had left had gone for gas, and now this fucking flat. Jusito'd better . . . That damn guy, nothing bothers him. Everything's a big laugh, and I believe he's going to die crazy. You never know what he's going to do, what he's going to come out with, what mess he's going to get into. And that fucking habit of goosing everybody every time you turn your back really bugs me. And the stupid things he says. But in any case, the fellow never wimps out on you. Better the guy backs me up tonight.

When Chale got to the drugstore, jumping puddles, Jusito was doubled over laughing, and Chale just let him get it out of his system.

"Uuuh, what a cool dude. Didn't you say the car and me and that and . . ."

"Never mind, it had more holes than you do, fucker."

"Well, that takes care of that. Now we're gonna be left with a hard . . ."

"And the chicks?"

"They're already inside. They've been waiting a long time. Come on, let's go, man. . . ."

"Hold on, dude. I'm broke. Not a . . ."

"Uuuh, what a guy. Here, dude, lookie here. Four big ones."

"Where from?"

"The batteries, dude. I don't think Johnny's tractors'll be starting tomorrow."

"All right, then. Wave to the chicks."

By the time they got to the theater, Jusito and Olga had French-kissed and he had her peeing her pants laughing. But Mary cut Chale dead for the way the guy had been misbehaving. So he gave her lots of bullshit like there was no other chick that made him feel as good as she did, and as soon as he had some dough he'd buy her a ring. Then he went on about how his old man

Teléforo did part-time chores for his boss because he could no longer handle the hard work and he himself had to help him out. He told her why he had stood her up the other day—the police'd caught him speeding and since he was stinking drunk, he'd fucked up when they made him stand on one foot. The police'd stripped him even of his underwear, and when he got out, he'd gotten mixed up in Betabel's shit over on the Other Side. In this way he'd calmed his woman down by the time they got to the movies.

Inside, they laughed and laughed at Tom and Jerry. But that's all they watched because by the time Tarzan started beating his chest, with the ape doing the same, the guys had their hands full and their eyes half cocked. They had a great time petting until Jane came on, and that's when the shit started. The guys didn't realize that their hands were in slow motion until they really stopped on the chicks' tits and paid attention. Hot damn, Jane was quite a piece! The chicks got jealous when they saw how their men were all gaping and they put up a stink. Mary told Chale not to be such a pig with his mouth hanging open, but Olga really got upset. She began to scream at them all kinds of dirty words at the top of her voice so that everyone could hear. They had no choice but to go outside and see how to patch things up. Then the four went back in, but everybody was all bent out of shape.

Halfway through the movie the women asked for something to drink just to be bitchy and spiteful, because they knew the dudes were totally broke. Chale didn't know what to answer, but blabbermouth Jusito, who'd promised to cover his eyes when Jane appeared, told Chale to go with him. He saw him laugh and wink. So when the guys went out, the chicks were left dreaming, and when the dudes took their time coming back, they thought they were really going to make it up to them. Surely they were going to bring Cokes and hamburgers and fries, the whole bit. Let 'em sweat, the bastards, so they won't think we're just any piece of ass, right, friend? Yep, you've always got to be firm with those bastards.

They were busy with those thoughts when the guys arrived and plopped down like they hadn't brought a thing. But Jusito set a bag of something on the floor, wrapped in his sweater.

"Where're the Cokes?"

"We've got something better, but you've got to be quiet, because it's a surprise."

"Stupid jerks, you brought sh . . ."

"For sure, right, buddy?"

"That's right, it's . . ."

"You'd better cut the crap. Show us what it is or we're leaving."

"You've got it. Ready, buddy?"

". . ."

"But you've got to close your eyes first. . . ."

When the chicks went along, Jusito raised the container of Kool-Aid and set it on Olga's legs, and when she opened her eyes, Jusito was already almost out the door. Chale also made tracks behind him, and they ducked in the restroom to keel over laughing. The attendant shoved them out because they wouldn't stop laughing. Outside, they continued doubled over with laughter with no thought for their dates. Besides, the night's so rotten the only thing pretty is the fucking sky. With bunches of stars all over the place.

THE DAY DAWNED like Independence Day come late. "The water went over the bridge! It already broke into the fields upstream! It went all over Colorao's fields!" The news spread until it reached every corner of Presidio. The landowners began to curse, yelling for whatever tractors and tools that could be saved. Workers soon began to straggle along, all upset and exhausted by the struggle they'd gone through. There was nothing else to be done; dikes, shovels, and sandbags, bales of alfalfa, and everything humanly thought of had been in vain. The water was rolling over the fields of cotton and late cantaloupe. The water sought room to spread out its stiff tentacles, and when it encountered obstacles larger than itself, it roared at them. Then it swept around them, as though in this way taking on the necessary strength to swallow them up and continue its destruction. The bosses, the owners, turned around, got in their cars, and, their wheels squealing, drove off in a rage. "This year you're not going to get out of the hole, brother, because you didn't insure your crop. They'll come for your new alfalfa packer, the Allis Chalmers and its hoe, also the International that you were using to till with." "Son of a bitch. When you want the fucking water, you don't get it and now . . . goddamn. And all that money I put into repairing the gin . . . all that fucking work for nothing."

All morning there's no end to the line of people going to Sam's Phillips 66. The people from the town come to tank up, getting ready to leave. There's nothing left to do here except shove off to New Mexico or Odesson. "Working for the petroleum companies is what pays the best." "Yes, but what the fuck do I know about machines, and you've got to know how to talk English for those jobs." "Naw, buddy, I know the fellow there, he's a great guy. I'll get you in." The older men who've spent their lives in the fields show up, but they only fill up and leave without a word. They're only thinking about the problems they're going to have away from home—the rent, the shortage of food, the money they're to earn, and what they're going to eat. Then they'll come back here broke. But at least you've stayed alive, right?

On the other side of the street, Nancy's Café is already starting to jump. One by one the trucks filled with the hats of boisterous men begin to arrive. Then Immigration Service jeeps. Only the antennaed car of the sheriff is missing. Between mouthfuls of ham and eggs with coffee: "Damn, you should've seen how the water toppled that tree like a shithouse; the water's pouring all over the fucking place at Johnny's. He tried to save his bulldozer but the bank caved in. That stupid Lencho just let 'er go and he jump off like a scared rabbit. . . . Well, gotta go see if them ole boys done as I told them to. Guess there's nothing else to do but start buyin' Mexican cattle. I hear this guy down by Los Mochis got purty good ones to sell. I'm gonna try and lease some of that Campbell property so I can fatten them carcasses. Six months'll do it. I hear they're paying pretty good prices for beef this year."

Ben, Jr. has another idea: "I'm going to the valley for three months. I'll take the trailers, and I'll get a contract to transport the harvest for Vernes, Inc., and that way I'll recoup a little. After the river goes down, I'll fix the land up and ask the government for a subsidy. The government pays me not to plant. Two hundred twenty thousand tax-free dollars just as a favor. What more can I ask for? Nothing more. That way, the land rests."

The thought makes him generous with the waitress, and he leaves her fifty cents.

"Have a good day, sir."

"You too, ma'am."

THAT MORNING, the old woman Vicke and Chonito got up early
with Marcela's cramps, and by the time the sun came out, the
house was jumping. The still unborn baby was jabbing hard, and
there was no way to stop him. "It must be the blow you got yesterday, Daughter. Don't worry, you've still got time," the woman
told her, trying to make her happy. Then she ran back and forth
between the kitchen and the living room with cups of mint tea
and buttered tortillas, but Marcela refused to eat. "I told you no!
I'm already stuffed. Take it away! I don't want it!"

Chonito left them talking. He went off to Teléforo's house.
When he got there, he found everybody gathered together. "Carlos's off to California, and I had to get his clothes together. The
old man also got up early to help, but what with the damp these
days, he hasn't felt well at all. You know how his rheumatism
bothers him." Serafina was speaking to Chonito as though he were
José's son. . . . It was to be expected. The kid loved his boss more
than his own father, and he spent more time here in Presidio than
in Ojinaga. Besides, his real father was only interested in the
money the boy brought home, and if he didn't, he shoved the
shoe box at him, saying, "Hit the street, shithead!" It was difficult
to become a clown on those occasions. To make the Americans
and the Mexican soldiers hanging around laugh. He just couldn't.
He also couldn't stand the other boys who, like insurance agents,
followed the poor gringo until his face turned red. When they had
got him, three or four hit the ground, looking for more than two
feet. And when they saw that the man was no freak, they sat
thoughtfully on their boxes. Blond man, earth's mystery, vital
fullness, won't you tell us your secret?

The situation had gotten bad the last week, because since José
had fled, there was no work. But Chonito had decided to suffer
the consequences. More important was the well-being of the
Uranga family. So right from the start he told Teléforo that he
should count on him to fill sandbags and put up dikes along the
river. "Take care of Marcela and Vicke as best you can," José had
told him. Let a few days go by and then on Saturday cross the
river to report whether the bastards have gone. I'll be at Bernabé's.
If anything urgent comes up, count on my compadre, Teléforo."

He kept his word. In the afternoon he went into town. He
went to the gas stations, he sat down outside the café, he walked

around the hotel, and he even strolled over to the bridge, running the risk they'd nab him. He remembered very well that José had barely crossed over when they'd shown up asking, "Where's José Uranga?" and when they didn't find him, they'd gone back. After a few days they were back in Presidio with an order to arrest him for avoiding the draft. Meanwhile, Chonito came and went with the news, until José at last had decided to move to the other side. He couldn't see himself killing people who shared no blame in the squabbles between politicians. "Talk to Teléforo and tell him to do me the favor tomorrow night. He already knows what he's got to do," he said to him.

Chonito had killed the first hours of the previous night under the soaking wet tents put up to celebrate the national holiday. He had waited until twelve o'clock among the games of dice, clothes raffles, and the shouting of drunks. Then, with the necessary courage, he had crept like a cat along the side of the bridge. Feeling his way, he'd found the boards, because the river was already flying high over them. After an eternal pulling at him, the current had let him cross. At two in the morning, Chonito was a wet shadow sneaking through the town, covered with mud. Then, a hot cup of tea, a woman wrapping him in a sheet, and a mattress stretched out on the floor. Chonito remembered nothing more.

"I only wanted to tell you that tonight is for what Don José asked you to do."

"Fine. Then tell Vicke that I will go for them right after sundown. In a little bit I'll tell Samuel to have the launch ready. But, go on, go have some lunch. Are you sure you don't want anything?"

"No, thanks. I already ate something on the other side. I'd better go see if there's something I can do."

"Okay, buddy, I'll be seeing you. Put 'er there."

"Take care of yourself over there."

"Sure, let's get going. Take care, okay?"

"You, too, Carlos."

THAT NIGHT THEY FOUND the river cresting with chocolate. It looked more like a dark mountain continuously rocking back and forth. Marcela, by contrast, thought about a hunched-up cat with its hair on end, opening its rabid maw without meowing. All she seemed to hear was a soft buzzing like a bumblebee off in the distance.

The woman lowers her head as if looking for something, as if her eyes could stop the sensation of something running down her legs. She feels a warm trickle that begins in the nerves of her head and runs down to her feet. But she doesn't say a thing. She only contemplates a mechanical scene, men in silence, running from the truck to the launch, tossing bundles that Vicke and Chonito had gathered together during the day. It seems that the whole scene is trapped in an enormous shell. Their nerves have turned into cords that cover their eyes, which is why they don't even realize it when light floods them. Not even when they are ready to help the women aboard the launch. Only when Teléforo returns to the truck does he notice the lights growing larger as they approach.

"Hurry up! Get into the launch; they're almost here!" he yells at them; at the same time he starts up the motor of his truck.

The launch man Samuel takes the little old woman in his arms, while Chonito grabs Marcela by the hand to make sure she doesn't trip. But they can't hear a thing. Their guts unclench.

Meanwhile, Teléforo waits for the lights to arrive. "I can take care of it myself. I'll tell them I've just come down to see the river, that's all. Those bastards know who I am. I'll tell them the launch's carrying two friends from Odessa whose mother's sick. That this is their car. What else can they ask? Yes, I'll wait for them here. . . . What? . . . It looks like they're turning the lights off. Who can it be?"

The man waits a moment longer, but nothing happens. He can barely make out the outlines of the car. Then he turns his truck around and drives over to where the lights had been. He drives by slowly, not able to believe there's no one there. He goes back again and then he goes down by the riverbank, but still nothing. He needs to see something, the lights, the outline at least. When he's convinced himself there's nothing, he turns toward home, confused. That's when he hears a loud blow against the windshield. The owl lies flapping its wings at the side of the road. But the man doesn't stop because the sound of the river has become the laughing of a giant. The devil returns to his beloved sierra.

THE FIRST PART of the crossing went by quickly, but the struggling of the launchmen became greater by the middle of the river, and

when the launch wouldn't go forward anymore despite their row-
ing like madmen, they let the water carry them for a while before
battling it again.

The little old woman squeezed her daughter's hand every time
the mountains of garbage collided with the launch, and she prayed
frantically to the saints. By contrast, Marcela's mind was like a
dead fish caught in a net. The pain came at intervals, a pain that
lasted one eternal minute and then disappeared like the ringing of
bells. She seemed suspended in air, beyond human feeling.

"How do you feel, Daughter?"

"Give me some water."

"There isn't any, Daughter."

"I want some water."

"Hold on just a little longer, my child."

Marcela closes her eyes and clamps her legs together as hard as
she can. It looks as if she's trying to remove the obstruction that's
between her legs.

"Take it away, Vicke."

"I can't, Daughter." The little old woman thinks Marcela's re-
ferring to the pain.

"I told you to take it away."

"Calm down, for God's sake, Daughter. You'll see it'll go away
soon."

The men row harder. The words of the women give them the
superhuman strength that, at another time, they might have run
out of. But it's not just that. Marcela's actions seem to indicate
that the woman is losing her mind because who in that state could
be indifferent to so much pain? No, it can't be natural, they think.

Nor what they now see. The limp body of the woman falls on
the little old woman, who screams, startled out of her wits, while
she clutches at her. But Marcela's not moving. The men quickly
forget about the launch and try to make her come to, but it's no
use. Only the dirty water is moving. The water and a newborn in
the middle of the river. Over the tops of the trees, over their
heads, some cottony clouds begin to wail.

Presidio 1970

O kay, just leave it like that, Son. Tomorrow we'll do a little bit more. We'd better turn in."

"Fine, Papa." And I stood up, putting the hoe over my shoulder.

The two of us walked silently, without speaking, toward the house. There was nothing for us to say. It seemed that the darkness pressed down on our exhausted and sweaty brains, leaving us mute. All you could hear was the grunt of clumps of dirt squashed by the feet of two exhausted men.

When will this all end? I thought, recalling the monotonous and eternal days. Tired days. Days without hope. Poor Papa. He's so old and he still doesn't realize that all the days are the same, without change. That everything boils down to life and death. Surely he hasn't even looked at himself well in the mirror, at the deep lines stamped on his face, at the curved stoop of yesterdays, at the fatigue reflected in his eyes of today.

"The sun sure was hot today, right, Son? It seemed like we were taking a sweat bath."

"Right. That's why I sat down for a good spell under the tree. After all, we weren't making much headway. There's no use in killing ourselves, right?"

He didn't answer. We fell silent again.

That's the way it's always been, Father. This damn land has always ended up with your blood, your sweat. And it hurts me that with every drop of your body part of your soul drains away, a life that is dying in order to live better. I know that your steps point day after day toward an emptiness, and I too am following them. But do you know why I'm doing it? For you, Papa. So you won't be left alone. But now I'm tired, Papa, and I haven't told you I'm leaving. I'm leaving because I'm certain that there's a world better than Presidio . . . Presidio, Texas. Even the name sounds sick to me because I first saw the light of day in Presidio, Texas, which, if you look at it, means under the tiled roof of the jailhouse.

"Tomorrow we'll go back to cleaning, right, Papa?"

"Yes, Son. There's still a little left to do. At least the rows that are going to get watered."

Sure, we'll put some more holes in our shoes, zigzagging like fools between the furrows. We'll pull out the weeds and we'll tramp and we'll walk, and there'll be another line on my old man's forehead. At

least right now we'll treat our fatigue with some rest in the emptiness
and darkness. Then, we'll get up early next morning as though time
had brought something new. As if time had boundaries. How stupid.
Life is measured only in terms of effort and action. How dumb are
those who consider us jackasses for having roots in "mañana land." But
they just don't understand that tomorrow means hope, that today you
worked fifteen hours, and that you hope to be able to withstand sixteen.
It's the hope of improving yourself, surpassing the limits of the body. It
never dies in Presidio. It asserts itself and nurtures like our daily bread,
to the point of becoming an eternal parasite. Yes, you've got to
hope. . . .

  "Why didn't you go to war, Father?"

  "Because I don't understand anything about squabbles between
countries. Why fight with others if the battle is here inside me, if hunger
is my own war? We, Son, are like a pair of dice that have been rolled
so much we've gotten round as marbles. And we won't stop rolling
until we find a niche. It's that niche we've got to battle and not against
ourselves."

  But the agents didn't hear you, don't you remember, Father? They
came and took you away to another jailhouse without a moment's hes-
itation, after you'd lost your wife. And now you're paying for the crime
of not having killed others, for not having become the enemy of your
own people. They refused to understand that for you the fight to live
was enough, and you had to serve the sentence. With four more lines
on your forehead, with two fallen wings, dragging along the ground,
with your back branded, don't you remember, Father? You came back
with your soul riddled and with a bleeding heart to walk these lands
again. And then you became worn out and got drunk and went mad
with the devil's laughter here in Presidio. And after I saw your tragedy,
I pulled myself from the clutches and left, do you recall? But now I've
come back, after a long time, and do you know why? Because you've
died. Yesterday we buried you at last in Presidio's dusty cemetery. I say
at last, because we'd grown weary of waking you, and I think you even
felt the same way. You must have been tired of being on display to so
many people, so much wailing. I only wanted to see you the first day.
Then I devoted myself to making the necessary arrangements and to
withstanding the condolences. Before then I hadn't realized how many
friends you had, all of them faces withered by time, and I thought that
life would kill them that way too, just like it did you. After the first day

of words like a broken record, I devoted myself to my grandmother Vicke. When I got here, I couldn't say a thing to her, so I let her get it out of her system against my chest, telling her clumsily not to cry. Then the two of us went over to contemplate the last vestiges of a scarred face, a face with fifty years of wrinkles and a heart beaten to death beneath the skin. "Life always scorned us." That's why I refused to come back to see you, because you died with your mouth making the same face of scorn. I'm certain that if you could've spoken to me at that moment, you would have scolded me. "Do you really think I'm going to let death make fun of me? Didn't I tell you to bury me with Mariachi music?" is what you would've said to me. But I also would have responded with the truth. Life played games with you, Papa. You died striking at your enemy and only hitting air. I know you couldn't avenge yourself. That's why you're bitter, Papa, because you were born with a smoking bitterness in Presidio, a pit of calcinated bones, in Presidio, "seven pierced letters in Holy Week, jailhouse of elongated time, a prison suspended in the steam of three o'clock in the afternoon, Presidio the joke, Presidio the unfortunate, Presidio born old." No, Don José, you don't have to ask for the children, they were born with wrinkles, at three in the afternoon. That's why there aren't, nor ever were, fevers in Presidio. People came into the world burned, melted down. The blood of their bodies was forged at one hundred twenty degrees. And that's why you loved and lived with your blood boiling—hatred was forged long before you died. And that bitterness from long ago has fastened onto me. I got it the first day we waked you. That's why I refused to see you again. Now, three days later, I feel better, although I've said goodbye to you forever. But, you know, I've decided to stay because we've got to remove the crown of thorns in Presidio. Yes, we've got to walk among the cactuses and the mesquites. We've got to endure the road, remove the crown, and put it on someone else. After that, we'll go down to the river and wash our wounds, and when we're clean, we'll return to Presidio, and if we want to keep on going, we'll have to come back strong, because we'll need the greatest willpower the soul has to give. Because they will see us and think we're mad and tell us to go preach down at the riverbank. The people who've put up with us will understand us, but they will not follow us because they'll be afraid, and there will be others who'll spit in our faces. They'll tell us everything's going fine, that the people are happy with their houses and jobs. But the miracle will take place, and then we'll have to bring them together, tell them about the devil that's gotten free and is still on the loose. They'll also have to be told about that famous fort that was born long before 1683 and about so many other things. Yes, we'll have to tell them, but not with suffering and with pardon. A flame has got to be lighted, the one that died with time.

About the Author

Aristeo Brito was raised in Southwest Texas. His poetry and short stories have appeared in numerous journals and anthologies, and his first collection, *Cuentos i poemas*, was published in 1974. The original Spanish-language edition of *El diablo en Texas* appeared in 1976. He has been actively involved in the promotion of Chicano literature in organizations such as the Modern Language Association, and he has lectured and read widely from his works throughout the United States and in Spain and Mexico. He has also received grants from the National Endowment for the Humanities and the National Endowment for the Arts. Brito received his Ph.D. from the University of Arizona in 1978, and he is presently Chairman of Languages at Pima Community College in Tucson, editor of *Llueve Tlaloc*, the college's bilingual literary magazine, and teacher of creative writing.